Go Up
the Road

Go Up
the Road

*Evelyn Sibley
Lampman*

ILLUSTRATED BY
CHARLES ROBINSON

A MARGARET K. MC ELDERRY BOOK

Atheneum   1972   New York

Some Other Books by the Same Author

CAYUSE COURAGE

THE YEAR OF SMALL SHADOW

Go Up
the Road

1

"IT IS DECIDED." Señor Ruiz finished the last of his tortilla. Then he looked at each of his children in turn. "Tomas, Yolanda, Roberto, Maria—you will inform your teacher that this is your last day in school."

Yolanda heard Papa's announcement with dismay. This was her third year in the fourth grade, and she was twelve years old. They always left before completing the term and returned after the next one had begun, so the teacher made her go back and start at the beginning. She wondered if she would ever pass into the fifth grade.

Lennie, who was only five and too young for school, asked the obvious question.

"Are we going up the road, Papa?"

"Yes, it is time to go up the road," he agreed.

"But not to California," said Mama quickly. "I will never again set foot in California."

Yolanda looked at her mother sympathetically. On other matters, Mama did not speak up to Papa this way, but in this one thing she was very firm. Last year, when they had been working in the grapes, Baby Carlos had sickened and died. They said it was the spray used to rid the vines of bad insects. The spray had been hard on all of them. Their skin itched, their eyes watered, and they coughed as though they would never stop, but on babies it was hardest of all. Finally, the angels took Carlos so he would not suffer any more.

In years past the angels had taken two other children from the family, but then there had been no known cause, and Mama accepted it. It was just something that happened. But Carlos' death was because of the spray, and Mama swore she would never go back to that place again.

"No." Papa frowned because good wives did not speak so to their husbands. "We do not go to California. There are strikes there. We must go where we can make enough money for the winter months, from December to April."

"You have signed with Juan Sanchez," said Tomas shrewdly. Tomas was fourteen, almost a man. Already, he could do a man's work in the fields. He was in the fifth grade and had announced that he would not go another year. This approach to manhood sometimes gave him courage to speak his mind. "I have read his posters in the Plaza and have heard him talk. He makes too many promises."

"*¡Calate!* Close your mouth!" Papa raised his voice, and he frowned at his eldest son. "The gringo schools have changed you into a boy without respect. They make us send our children there, then they teach them bad manners. What do you know of Juan Sanchez? Nothing! You are too young. Your father and the other men of Tierra Agreste will do the judging. Juan Sanchez is a stranger, but he is of our race. He knows our problems. He has come to help us."

Yolanda watched her brother's face redden under the rebuke. If only Tomas would remember that Papa was Papa and wait for him to give his opinion first.

"It is true that Juan Sanchez has made promises." Papa spoke to the others, ignoring Tomas. "And he has a fine truck. As labor contractor, he gives us free transportation. Think of that! Señor Matta will drive his own truck, and Juan Sanchez will pay for the gasoline and give him something more besides. There will be free houses when we arrive, fine houses with running water. There will be showers and washing machines so Mamacita need not scrub the clothes by hand. There will be free doctors and dentists. All of us will have our teeth fixed, and it will cost us nothing. There is free care for babies and for those like Lennie, who are too young to go to the fields. There is a free school, too, for children under nine. It is held in the summer, and Juan Sanchez says those who attend will not fall behind with their winter classes. Maria may go to that sometimes. Seven is too young for many of the crops. What she could pick would bring in very little."

Everything sounded very fine as Papa told it, thought Yolanda. How wonderful it would be for Maria not to fall behind in school. She looked at Tomas reproachfully, wondering why he was so mistrustful.

"Where is this place which promises such fine things?" asked Mama. She had been smiling ever since she heard about the washing machines.

"In Oregon."

"Oregon?" Mama's voice was startled. "Have you forgotten that Luis lives in Oregon? But perhaps you have forgiven him?"

"I have made enquiries," Papa told her stiffly. "Juan Sanchez says Oregon is a big place. I told him the name of the village where Luis lives. We will not go near there. Luis will not even know we are there. When he left home and married that girl from East Los Angeles, my father disowned him. Luis was so infatuated with a pretty face that he put his family behind him. Without a doubt, the woman has led him a fandango ever since."

"Aunt Minda says Uncle Luis is doing well," said Tomas softly. "She hears from him all the time. He is a logger and cuts down trees. She says he makes lots of money."

"¡Cálate!" Papa's voice came out in a great roar that echoed against the adobe walls. "I do not wish his name used in this house. He is no longer a son of my father, and he is no brother of mine. The first loyalty of a man is to his family, and Luis did not remember that. Therefore, he is no longer one of us."

Gentle little Maria broke the uncomfortable silence, and Yolanda looked at her gratefully. Maria hated unpleasantness, and because she was Papa's favorite, she usually managed to turn his anger.

"It will be nice to go to a school in summer," she said. "Will we leave for Oregon tomorrow, Papa?"

"We leave tomorrow, but not for Oregon," he told her. "The crops in Oregon will not be ready until June. First we go to Utah for the celery."

"But now you go to school," said Mama briskly, getting to her feet. "Tell the teacher it is the last day, as Papa said. And hurry home. There will be much to do to get ready."

She gave each child a quick inspection at the door, examining faces, hands, and ears. Their clothes might be worn, there might even be a few holes, but there was no excuse for dirt. Not everyone in the village was as particular as Mama about dirt, and sometimes the boys complained about it. They said that her scrubbing was peeling their skin away and that when they were grown they would never wash except on fiestas. But Yolanda was glad that Mama

7

felt that way. She would be ashamed to run around like the Naranja children, with running noses and clothes that smelled.

Her brothers rushed ahead, but Yolanda lingered in the thin sunlight of early morning. The air was cold, and she wrapped her rebozo around her more closely.

"Do you want me to wait for you?" asked Maria.

"No. Go on with the others. I want to talk with Rosie," Yolanda told her. She was almost sure that Rosita Corona and her family would be going to Oregon, but she had to find out.

From almost every house, children were rushing out into the dusty street. They were excited because it was the last day of school.

Yolanda shivered. Her old brown rebozo was getting very thin and no longer kept out the cold. She wished she had a new one, thick and preferably red. A thick rebozo might make her look fatter. People wouldn't always make those remarks about a heavy wind blowing her away. And a red one might reflect some of its color in her light tan cheeks. It might even make her look a little pretty. Yolanda didn't think anything about her was pretty now. Her face was narrow, and her eyes were too large. Roberto always said they looked like brown goggles. But at least there was nothing wrong with her hair. It was dark and thick, and she wore it in braids like all the other girls.

She walked a short way down the unpaved street, stopping in front of the third small adobe. All the houses in Tierra Agreste, a village in New Mexico, looked alike. They were small, three-room adobes, unpainted—for paint cost money—and each sat side by side on plots of land thirty feet square. There was just room along the sides for a few rows of chilis, beans, or corn. The village had one church and one small store, which also doubled as a *cantina,* and a dusty plaza, where the people could gather on special occasions. The largest building was the school, built by the government, which all the children had to attend until they claimed to be sixteen. It was not a pretty town and had arisen from necessity.

Yolanda could not remember another home, but her parents had told her of the time when the Ruiz family owned land. It was only ten acres, but compared with thirty feet that was a great deal. Grandfather Ruiz and his father before him had raised cattle, allowing them to roam free through the vast acres of common land that once belonged to everyone.

The first Ruiz had been living here when all this country belonged to Mexico, not the United States. After the war between those nations, a treaty had been signed. That was in 1848, and it said that the Mexicans already living there were now American citizens.

For several years things continued as always, but

the new Mexican-Americans stayed by themselves as much as possible. They clung to their old customs, the Spanish language, and to each other. It was the only thing they could do. They were resented by the new settlers, the Anglo-Americans, who now swarmed into the country. The Anglos wanted the land for themselves. They called the Mexican-Americans "greasers," and sometimes they shot them just for fun.

After Grandfather died, the farm belonged to Yolanda's father, but he could not keep it. Every year there were mounting taxes and water bills he could not pay. His cows died, and the land was too poor to farm. Besides there was no money for tools or seed. He lost the farm, and they moved to Tierra Agreste, where others of similar background had gathered. Most of them became migrants. Every year from April through November, they traveled, working the fields of strangers. Then they returned home, doling out their savings, subsisting until the next harvest.

Yolanda wished it didn't have to be that way. She wished they had a home with land enough to grow more than a few rows of chili and corn and the money to farm it—a home they would never have to leave, where there was enough to eat and where she could complete a whole year in school.

She glanced impatiently toward the Corona's front door. They were slow this morning. If they didn't hurry she would have to go on alone. She didn't want to be late on her last day of school.

Then the door opened, and Rosita rushed out, followed by her five younger brothers. Although she was no taller than Yolanda, Rosita was more solidly built. Her face was round, and her hair was pulled back so smoothly into its two braids that it looked like a shiny black cap. From her chin to the middle of her bare muscular legs, she was wrapped in a faded green rebozo, and on her feet were tennis shoes so snug that each toe was outlined through the cloth.

"Did you hear? Did your papa tell you?" she shouted. "We are going to Oregon tomorrow, but first we go to Utah for the celery."

Yolanda breathed a sigh of relief. Rosie was going! They would not be separated.

"He told us." Then she frowned. "Talk English. Now we go to school."

Speaking English on the way to school was something they did each morning. Spanish was not permitted in the classrooms, and Yolanda had convinced Rosie that if they began using the more difficult language a few minutes early, it would give them a head start on the others.

"Today is the last day of school." Rosie continued to speak in Spanish, and her face took on a stubborn look. "English is a waste of time. A stupid idea. No matter how hard we try, the teacher complains that we do not say it right. She wants us to talk like book reading. Nobody talks that way."

"The teachers talk that way," said Yolanda in English. She glared at her friend angrily. If the idea had been Rosie's, there would be no argument. Rosie always wanted to be the leader.

"Only because they are teachers," Rosie pointed out triumphantly. "They would not otherwise. I am glad we are through with school for awhile. I hate school. It is dull."

Yolanda did not answer. On the subject of school, she and Rosie never agreed. It was better not to discuss it, but she wasn't going to admit that her idea was stupid. Rosie didn't always have to be right. She could just keep on talking Spanish, and Yolanda would speak English. They would see who gave in first.

"Will Señor Sanchez take to Oregon Tierra Agreste all?" she asked, being careful to include all the small unwieldy English words, though perhaps they were not in the right order.

"All but those who accept welfare money from the government," answered Rosita, still in Spanish. "The Widow Huerta and the Naranjas will stay here as always. They might lose their money if they worked."

It was a great disgrace to go on welfare, not that there weren't government agents around urging people to do so.

"*Los pobrecitos,*" said Yolanda scornfully, then

13

bit her lip.

Rosie grinned triumphantly. Now that she had won, she was willing to speak English for the remainder of the walk to school. "We make fun. We no been to Oregon and Utah."

"Will it different much from California?" asked Yolanda ruefully. It was too bad the Spanish words had slipped out, but it was over now and best forgotten.

"Sure. No grapes. No lettuce. No oranges. Señor Sanchez say after celery, we pick berries and cucumbers and beans. Three months, all in same place. Then we pick apples, and last the potatoes."

"Good," said Yolanda automatically, but she really didn't think so. Through her mind floated a vision of hundreds of wooden crates, loaded with red berries and green cucumbers, and rows of gunny sacks, knobby with string beans. She had never picked apples or potatoes, so she couldn't picture them, but she was sure they would mean hard work, too.

It was starting all over again.

2

"I HOPE I LIKE better Oregon than Utah," said Rosie. She didn't speak very loudly, for any father who overheard might think she was complaining. Grownups could complain and very small children, but complaints from a twelve-year-old were better left unsaid.

"Here it has sun," Yolanda reminded her, peering over Roberto's head through the back opening of the truck. "I no think I would get warm again."

She hoped they would never go back to Utah. Not only had she been cold, but in the beginning she was always a little hungry. Juan Sanchez said they must be there by the first of April, and they were; but when they arrived the celery wasn't ready. For two weeks they waited, shivering in the drafty shacks provided for the workers. They had eaten as sparingly as possible, since the money paid for food had to be advanced by the labor contractor and paid back to him. Only Mama had not complained about the sparseness of their meals.

"I am too fat now," she always explained, when anyone spoke of how slowly she finished each meal. "Like a bear, I could live on my fat all winter. With you *niños* it is different. You are growing and must eat. Have the other half of my tortilla. I cannot force down another mouthful."

Mama's appetite improved when they began being paid for their work, but by then there were other worries. Yolanda knew all about them, because such things were discussed openly.

The money they received from Juan Sanchez was very little. They had not known food would be so expensive, and there were other costs as well. Although transportation was supposed to be free, Sanchez explained that would be true only had they gone straight to Oregon. He could not be expected to finance their side trip to Utah. The charge had to come out of their earnings.

There had been rent to pay on the cabins, and something called Social Security was taken out. Yolanda did not know what that was, but it had something to do with the government. Juan Sanchez said they would get it back when they were sixty-five, but who would live so long?

The weather warmed before they finished with the celery, but the memory of those first early weeks stayed with them. Yolanda was sure she would never see celery again without thinking of cold winds and icy rain. They were all glad to be going up the road once more.

This morning before daybreak, their possessions had been loaded into the two trucks, and the older people had taken places on the hard benches that were built around three sides of the back. The children had squeezed in between the boxes and bundles on the floor. Both trucks were covered, so their only view was through the back opening.

There was so much quarreling about who should sit close to the tailgate that the mothers had scolded sharply. The bickering ceased, but the children had taken their usual small revenge. All morning they had spoken nothing but English. Most of the fathers could understand English, but few of the mothers knew more than a word or two. It was exasperating for them to hear from their children a babble of sounds with no meaning.

"We make stop at town," announced ten-year-old Roberto. He and his friend Albert Corona had managed to get the best places at the tailgate.

"How you know it is town?" demanded Albert.

"I see sign," shrieked Roberto. "It say, 'Thank you. Come again.' Why we stop you think?"

"The troka no *función* if it no have gasoline," Tomas reminded him in a superior tone. He was angry because the fourteen-year-olds had been told to sit on the floor with the other children. Yolanda preferred the floor, and she thought Tomas did too. He only wanted to sit on a bench because they were for adults.

"I wish we could get out," she whispered to Rosie. "I got the crick bad in my back."

Rosie shrugged. Everyone knew that the occupants must remain in the truck during gas stops. A crick in the back was something that had to be endured.

Yolanda pushed past Roberto to look at the town. It was very small, not more than half a dozen houses. There was only one store with a gas pump in the front.

The truck, driven by Juan Sanchez, was serviced first, then it pulled ahead and waited while Señor Matta drove the second truck to the pump.

At the side of the building, next to the pump, were signs reading "Men" and "Ladies." When she saw them, Maria squeezed through the crowded truck and whispered in her mother's ear. Mama shook her head firmly. Migrants were not welcome in public restrooms.

"No importa," Yolanda told her, when Maria had squirmed back to her place. "It is pretty soon twelve o'clock. We got to stop then. That is the law. Señor Sanchez will stop where there is trees and bushes."

How nice it would be, Yolanda thought, to walk up and ask the service station attendant for the key, and then boldly enter a public restroom as the gringos did. She wondered what the inside of a restroom looked like. She had never seen one.

After they left the town, the cultivated fields on either side were soon replaced by uncleared land. They drove through scattered woods, which soon gave way to thicker trees. The highway wound up and up, and the truck was forced to reduce speed. Finally Señor Sanchez turned off the paved highway onto a narrow dirt road that had been cut through the trees, and Señor Matta followed. It was rough, and the truck jolted up and down through the ruts, stirring up a cloud of dust. The road curved, and almost immediately the highway was hidden from view.

The people in the truck smiled at each other, and the children stopped speaking English and reverted to the familiar Spanish. They pushed each other aside to see out the back, and this time the mothers ignored them tolerantly.

It was a good feeling—a secure feeling—thought Yolanda, of being in a world where everyone else was shut out. Even the whiz of fast, expensive motors speeding along the hidden highway was muted. She wished they could stay a long time in this secret place that smelled of pine trees and warm dust.

As soon as they came to a stop, everyone began scrambling over boxes and bags in an effort to get to the ground. Yolanda stretched to get rid of the

crick in her back; others were doing the same. Outside of a short rest stop in mid-morning, they had
been traveling since sun-up.

"We stop here thirty minutes," shouted Juan
Sanchez. "That is the law, and I am a good labor
contractor. I do everything the law says. Do not all
adults get benches to sit on? Not like the old days
when you used to be packed in like potatoes in a
sack. This is an old fire road, and it is quiet. The
Anglos do not use it much. I do not want any of you
muchachos wandering off. Stay here, so you will be
ready when it is time to leave."

"What is a fire road?" asked Yolanda. "Does it
lead to a fire?"

The narrow dirt road curved into the forest, and
she could not see the end. It would be fun to walk
on and on, and never have to come back to Señor
Sanchez and his jolting truck.

"*¿Que le hace?* Who cares?" said Rosie. She
stomped up and down. "The devil has poured sand
over my foot. It has gone to sleep."

The pines grew high above their heads, and the
ground below was clear of undergrowth. They
wandered among the trees, picking up huge cones
that had fallen from the branches. Yolanda wanted
to take some with her, but Rosie convinced her they
were useless. They were good only for making fires,
and undoubtedly the camp would have butane gas.

One of the boys found a little mountain stream

that trickled through a gully, and everyone had a long drink of the clear, cold water. Señor Sanchez hadn't known about the stream, and Yolanda could tell that he wasn't pleased. It was probably because people preferred the cold water to the tepid coke he carried in the truck and sold at lunch and rest stops. He herded them back into the trucks as soon as he could, and because no one else owned a watch, everyone was sure he had cut their noon time short.

There was some grumbling about that, but most of the conversation was about another announcement the labor contractor had made during the stop. They would not continue on to the camp where they were to spend three months. He had phoned ahead, and the raspberries were not ripe. It was his idea that they stop on the way and pick strawberries. He had not made arrangements for this, but he was sure he could find a grower who would hire them.

When he finished speaking, Yolanda looked at her father. Papa and the other men would decide whether or not to accept this change of plans. Only on rare occasions would the women voice an opinion; the children, of course, would do as they were told.

"At least it is better than it was with the celery," said Papa. "We will not be sitting around, eating up money we have not earned."

"It is piecework only. They will pay by the crate," Señor Corona reminded him glumly.

"Even so, it is something," insisted Papa. "Strawberries make a good crop for children. It is easy for them to crawl on the ground."

Yolanda winced inwardly. By the end of the season, when her knees were calloused, crawling on the rough ground wasn't bad. But the first crop was always hard.

"I cannot get down to pick strawberries," said Antonia Galindez, as her husband helped her into the truck. "My stomach is too fat with the baby."

"Then you must stay with me," Grandmother Corona told her. "I too cannot get on my knees. We will look after the small children together."

"When will Tonia's baby be born?" Yolanda whispered to Rosita.

"In three months time. She is very frightened." Rosie glanced toward the bench where her older sister had found a seat. Antonia's cotton dress strained against her swollen body, and she clutched the hand of her young husband, Pablo Galindez, very tightly.

Yolanda thought of their wedding. It had taken place last fall, when everyone returned to Tierra Agreste. Because there was money from the harvest in his pocket, Señor Corona had given his eldest daughter a fine fiesta, with much to eat and drink and dancing through the night. Antonia had a new white dress and had worn flowers in her hair. She looked so beautiful, and Pablo had been so proud and handsome. She didn't look beautiful now, only uncomfortable and much older. It was hard to believe that Tonia was only fifteen.

Eventually they reached the top of the mountain range and began going down. Yolanda could tell that was so because she had to brace herself to keep from sliding. The trees along the road changed from pine to fir, and they could look out the back and see great unbroken expanses of trees going on and on in the valley below. They grew so closely that it looked as though she could walk across their tops without falling in. She wondered if they would feel solid under her feet or tickle her toes.

"What are you smiling about?" demanded Rosie.

"Nothing," said Yolanda quickly. It didn't do to tell Rosie such thoughts. Rosie said she was crazy to make up things.

"My Uncle Luis is a logger. He cuts down trees like those," announced Roberto. "Here in Oregon, too."

"Hush," cautioned Yolanda. "Papa will hear."

"How do you know?" asked Albert. "You have never even seen your uncle."

"My Aunt Minda, in East Los Angeles, sees him," explained Roberto. "She told Mama about it last year, and I was listening. She wishes Papa and Uncle Luis would make up their quarrel. She says it is silly. It is not as though Uncle Luis had married a gringo. She is Mexican-American like us."

This time Yolanda leaned over and twisted Roberto's ear. It was the only way to make him stop.

When the highway skirted the foot of a tall snow-covered mountain, Señor Matta stopped the truck so people could take turns looking out the back. It was truly something to see. Grandmother Corona, who had been in Mexico, said it reminded her of Popocatepetl, the great snowy peak beyond Mexico City. Of course, she added, this mountain was not nearly so fine as old Popo.

This one looked very large to Yolanda, and she did not see how old Popo could be any finer. She wondered what it would be like to climb to the very top of such a mountain. What a view she would have! She would see for hundreds of miles in every direction. The ascent did not look very difficult—if she just had time, she was sure she could make the climb. It would be exciting to stand on the very peak and wave a flag so all the people below could see.

"I would like to climb that mountain and stand on the very top," she told Rosie impulsively.

"What for?" asked Rosie in surprise. "There is nothing up there but snow."

Soon after they left the mountain behind, the trees began thinning out. There were occasional small settlements set back from the highway, and for a time a noisy white river raced beside them. Then they came to farmlands, and Señor Sanchez turned off the highway onto a graveled side road.

"Where are we now?" asked Rosie, but she didn't

expect anyone to answer her question.

They appeared to be on a quiet country road that went up and down gentle hills. On the left were pastures, studded with occasional trees and bushes, but the right side was under cultivation. Row after row of leafy plants hugged the ground. They went on for what looked to Yolanda like miles and miles.

"Strawberries," said Roberto unnecessarily. Everyone in the truck knew what they were.

"I wish I had some now," said Albert. "I have great hunger."

"You will have to wait until tomorrow," Roberto reminded him. "The owner will not let you go into the fields to help yourself."

"I know," agreed Albert sadly. "Last year when we finished, I did not want to look at another strawberry as long as I lived. Now they sound pretty good."

Eventually Señor Sanchez drove into the yard of a modern farmhouse. Its many windows glittered in the orange light of the setting sun, and there was a television antenna on the roof and a double garage with two cars inside. The labor contractor motioned to Señor Matta to wait while he himself got out of the first truck and went to the back door. After a moment it was opened by a woman wearing blue slacks and a white blouse.

Yolanda wondered who the woman was. She was probably the maid. Anyone who owned so fine a house would not answer the back door dressed in slacks. She would wear silk and lace, with jewels hanging from her ears and neck.

Finally the woman pointed to the pasture land across the road. Then she closed the door, and Señor Sanchez returned. He went first to the back of Señor Matta's truck, where he spoke to the people in a loud, clear voice.

"It is your great fortune that I know this grower," he said. "He is not at home, but I talked with his wife."

His wife! Yolanda could hardly believe it. A fine house, two cars—yet the owner's wife wore pants like a man! Surely the gringos were very odd.

"They have confidence in me, and when I say I bring only the best pickers, they take my word for it," continued Señor Sanchez. "They pay ninety cents for every crate picked, and of course, you must give me ten since I procured the job for you. Not all growers around here have cabins, but this one does. The cabins are very cheap. Three dollars and a half a week is all you must pay."

A murmur of appreciation came from the occupants of the benches. Even Yolanda, who never saw any of the money she earned by picking crops, realized that this was a bargain. Migrant cabins often ran as high as fifteen dollars a week.

She had been keeping her eyes on the beautiful house, and now she saw the back door open again. A moment later the owner's wife stepped outside and started across the yard. As she drew nearer, she looked even less like a great lady, for her red hair was done up in knobby rollers all over her head.

"Mr. Sanchez," she called as she drew closer. "There's one more thing I forgot to tell you."

"Yes, Mrs. Truaxe." Señor Sanchez whirled quickly. He seemed surprised and started forward to meet her.

Mrs. Truaxe, however, had caught sight of the children's faces in the back of the truck, and she walked right past him.

"Hello there." She stopped next to the tailgate, smiling warmly. "So you're our new pickers. I'm sure you're very fast, all of you."

There was no mistaking the friendliness of her smile, and some of Yolanda's disappointment began to fade. Even though she wore pants instead of a silk dress and appeared in hair rollers, Mrs. Truaxe seemed like a nice lady. Yolanda wished she could think of something to say, but no words came to her. She could only smile shyly.

Rosie felt no such hesitation.

"I am the fastest," she boasted. "I pick as much berries as some man."

Yolanda felt herself blushing for her friend. Behind her she could hear disapproving sounds from the fathers on the benches. It wasn't polite of Rosie to say such things, even if they were true.

27

"Good for you," declared Mrs. Truaxe approvingly.

"You wished to tell me something, Mrs.?" said Señor Sanchez.

"Oh, yes." She turned to him, mindful of the errand that had brought her outside. "About the firewood. We furnish that too, as well as the cabins. They're both free. So tell your people to help themselves to all they need."

Everyone heard her, but Tomas was the first to recover his voice.

"The cabins they are free, Señora?" he asked.

"Why, yes," said Mrs. Truaxe in surprise. "Didn't your contractor tell you? They're not much, but at least they won't cost you anything." She smiled again at the now astonished faces in the truck, then turned to go. "I hope you can pick lots of berries," she called. "Be sure to pick the vines clean."

"I was mistaken," Señor Sanchez assured them quickly, but Yolanda noticed that a red flush was creeping up from his neck. "The señora did not say before that the cabins were free, any more than she mentioned the firewood. Last year, when we were here, there was a charge; I assumed it was the same. It was a natural error."

Without another word, he walked back to the first truck and climbed into the driver's seat.

Yolanda wondered if it really was a mistake. Tomas wouldn't think so. He had mistrusted the labor contractor from the beginning, and now she agreed with him. Señor Sanchez was no better than a *bandido!* He was stealing their money right from under their very noses.

As they bumped over the rough road, she could hear the others arguing about it, too. Was it really a misunderstanding, or had Juan Sanchez meant to cheat them? He was a stranger. They had taken him on trust because of his fine truck and many promises. There was the matter of the transportation charges to Utah. Had those also gone into the man's pocket?

Yolanda began imagining Tomas and herself exposing the *bandido* to all the people of Tierra Agreste. Just how they had managed to bring it about would take a little more thought, but the final scene was very easy. Sanchez was on his knees, praying for forgiveness, while she and Tomas stood by, pointing scornful fingers. All the townspeople were cheering, and Papa and Mama were smiling proudly.

"You have that funny look on your face that you get sometimes," accused Rosie, pulling on her arm.

Yolanda came back with a start.

"I cannot help the way I look," she protested.

"The cabins are just ahead," said Rosie, unconvinced. "It will be a long walk back up the hill from the fields."

The cabins were on the far side of the pasture, well hidden from the road. It would be a mile's walk

to the fields each morning and another mile back when they were tired. They were under a grove of spreading maple trees, which would be protection from the sun on hot days. But even before Señor Matta turned off his engine, Yolanda knew that this was going to be a bad camp.

Roberto put her own feelings into words.

"It stinks," he said, holding his nose.

3

THE SOURCE OF THE SMELL was not hard to locate. Garbage was heaped outside the cabins, and flies hummed noisily as they flew from one pile to another. The buildings themselves were small—perhaps nine feet square—made of unpainted, weathered lumber. Each had a single door, but there were no windows.

Spaced in front of every two cabins was a rusty cook stove with a pile of firewood beside it. Next to that was a rough picnic table, with benches attached to two sides. Fires were already burning in a few of the stoves, for some of the cabins were occupied.

As the trucks jolted to a stop, the women who were tending the fires looked up briefly, then, without interest, they continued preparing the evening meal. The children, however, were more curious than their mothers. They stopped their play to stand and stare openly at the newcomers. Yolanda inspected them quickly. They were all Indians.

The group from Tierra Agreste mumbled angrily as they climbed from the trucks. They had seen bad camps before, but this was one of the worst. It was not fit for cattle, much less people.

"Remember, it is free," called Señor Sanchez hastily. "There will be no charge. Everyone is supposed to bury his garbage. I will speak to the owner and tell him that those who are here are not doing so. He will see that they do, and then the smell will go away. You will find water faucets at intervals throughout the camp, and the water here is good. Cool and without the taste of minerals. There are privies out in back. Six or eight of them, if I remember right. As you heard, firewood is free. Choose a cabin next to your best friend, then you can share a stove, and the preparation of your meals will be pleasant. It will be like a fiesta."

The people of Tierra Agreste looked at him, saying nothing.

"There are no lines for electricity," said Rosie in a low voice.

Yolanda nodded. "There will be nothing to do but go to bed after supper."

Slowly and with set faces, the women began advancing toward the cabins, opening doors. Each cabin contained two double beds, built against the wall, with moldy springs and mattresses. There was room for nothing else.

33

Yolanda followed her mother to the door of one of the cabins and peered around her into the dark interior. It smelled musty and close.

"I would rather sleep outside, Mamacita," she said quickly.

"It would not be proper for a young girl to sleep in the open," her mother reminded her firmly. "Tomas and Roberto will sleep under the trees. You, Maria, and Lennie will have one of the beds. Now help me get these mattresses outside. We must sun them as much as we can before it is too dark."

As she helped her mother carry the mattresses outside, Yolanda asked herself why they bothered. They were just trading the musty odor for the smell of someone's garbage.

The next morning they were in the fields before six o'clock. The walk had been pleasant, for once they left the camp the air was fresh and smelled of clean earth, warming under the sun, and of new grass and wild flowers. There was a little pond, fed by a small stream that ran through the pasture, and Albert and Roberto had a great discussion about whether it might contain fish. They planned to try it out that evening.

Yolanda was surprised when Juan Sanchez called the tall, sandy-haired man, who seemed to be in charge of the field, Mr. Truaxe. Usually they never saw the owner of the crops they picked, only his overseer. This owner was different. He assigned rows, checked crates, and punched tickets himself. He seemed nice enough, even if his camp was one of the worst they had lived in.

"I'm glad you started early," he told them. "I've got a couple of busloads of school kids coming out from town to pick. You'll be underway by the time they get here."

Yolanda and Rosie exchanged glances. Gringo children could be very unpleasant. They had met only a few, for the camps were usually filled with Mexican-Americans like themselves, and a few blacks. Sometimes, as in this camp, there were Indians, but their children were usually shy. By the time they had warmed up enough to be friendly, they were ready to move on. Only a few gringo families were migrants, and neither Yolanda nor Rosie had liked their children. They were rude and loud. They never bothered to wash when they returned from the fields, and they wrote dirty words on the washroom walls. Now Mr. Truaxe said there would be a whole busload of them working in the fields.

"Dirty gringos!" said Rosie under her breath. "Why do they come here?"

"They may not even look at us," Yolanda told her reassuringly. She hoped that's what would happen. Gringo children stared. They didn't smile. They just stared, as though she were a curiosity.

Yolanda and Rosie asked for rows side by side and

were almost the last to be assigned. It brought them very close to where the gringo children would work. Only Roberto and Albert, who shared a row, would be closer.

"Pick fast and get far ahead," advised Rosie, dropping to her knees. "The fumble-fingered gringos can never catch up."

It was good advice. Yolanda placed her empty crate on the shady side of the row and crouched down, her fingers searching out the red berries hiding among the wide, green leaves.

She worked as fast as she could, but the first picking, as usual, was slow. Not all the berries were ripe, and sometimes one side of the same berry would be red while the other side was white. That meant extra time, since the grower would be angry if she wasn't careful to put the white side downward in the box. It would take over an hour to fill the twelve boxes in the crate, but as Papa said, it was better than nothing. Except for Lennie, who had stayed in camp with Grandmother Corona and Antonia, the whole family had come to the fields. If the berries held out, their combined efforts would put some money into the winter horde.

"Here they come," announced Rosie in a loud whisper.

A yellow bus had pulled up at the edge of the field. Yolanda looked over her shoulder. She was glad they had a head start. By now she and Rosie were well down the row.

The field, which had been quiet, now echoed to the shouts of the children getting off the bus. There were a frightening number of them, thought Yolanda, boys as well as girls. As near as she could tell, they ranged in age from about ten to fifteen, and they carried lunch buckets or bulging sacks. They were all laughing and talking, running this way and that, having a gay time. Yolanda turned back to the berries hastily.

There was a shrill, piercing sound behind her, and she looked again. A large woman in brown overalls and a straw hat was blowing a whistle. Her cheeks puffed out with the effort, and it made her look funny. All the gringo children gathered around her. The woman spoke to them a moment, then Mr. Truaxe began assigning rows.

Unlike the Mexican Americans who were given a row apiece, or at most shared it with one other picker, these children were spaced several along each row. When a picker reached the point where his predecessor had begun, he skipped ahead beyond the last worker in a row. This brought the third picker very close to the place where Yolanda was working.

"Remember to pick clean." Mr. Truaxe shouted as loudly as he could. "Don't leave ripe berries, and don't pick the green ones. Don't pull on the vines or yank at them."

He hadn't given those instructions to the people

from Tierra Agreste. There had been no need to, Yolanda thought scornfully. They knew how to handle fruit.

"There's a barrel of drinking water back here close to the bus," shrieked the lady with the whistle. "Don't waste it. Mr. Truaxe had to haul it all the way out here. And I don't want anybody throwing dirt clods or berries. You're here to work, remember."

There were three girls spaced at intervals on the row next to Albert and Roberto. One was at the very beginning, the second was placed six feet beyond her, while Mr. Truaxe told the third to move up even farther. Yolanda deliberately turned her back and tried to concentrate on the berries. It was hard to do now, for the newcomers made a great deal of noise. From behind came snatches of conversation, laughter, and music from a radio someone had brought to the field. Obviously, the children all knew each other, and the berry picking was a game, an outing almost like a fiesta. It made her feel like an outsider, even though Rosie was picking steadily on the next row, and the people of Tierra Agreste were silently working in the same field.

"Hi." The voice came from behind her, and it was quite close. Yolanda looked over her shoulder. The third girl on the row next to Albert's and Roberto's was standing there, smiling at her.

"Hi," said Yolanda timidly. The girl looked

friendly enough, but you couldn't tell about these things. Not at first. She was short, with a round face and blue eyes. Her brown hair was long, and she had fastened it back with two lengths of ribbon. She wore jeans, cut off at the knees, and a plaid shirt.

"My name's Kim. Kim Grant. I'm from South School. We all are. What's your name?"

"Yolanda Ruiz." She repeated it slowly to make sure the girl heard the Spanish pronunciation, *E-o-landa*. Once, in a strange gringo school, the teacher had asked her to spell it first. After that everyone called her "Yo," and sometimes "Yo-yo," like the toy that went up and down on a string. She didn't want that to happen again.

"Where you from, Yolanda?" Kim had been listening. She said it correctly.

"New Mexico."

"That's a long way off. I've never been there. I've only been in Oregon and Washington and California. We went to Disneyland last summer. Have you ever been there?"

"No," said Yolanda wistfully. Disneyland wasn't too far from East Los Angeles, where Aunt Minda lived, but it was very expensive. Aunt Minda said ten dollars went just like that in Disneyland, and with seven in the family, it wouldn't be a drop in the bucket. She turned back and began putting berries in her box.

"Well," said Kim cheerfully. "I better get to work.

I'm going to buy a new camera with my berry money. The kind that develops a picture in sixty seconds. I just love to take pictures, don't you?"

Yolanda agreed that she loved to take pictures, and it wasn't quite a lie. She had never taken one—no one in Tierra Agreste owned a camera—but she was sure she would love it if she had the chance. For a moment she wondered what it would be like to spend the money she earned for anything she wanted. Then she put the thought from her mind. Such a thing could never be. She shifted her position, picking from the side of the row, so she could glance across at this friendly gringo from time to time.

Kim was having a difficult time getting into a comfortable position to pick. She knelt on her bare knees, but the ground was hard and lumpy. She tried crouching over the vines, but almost immediately she gave that up. Finally she sat down, scooting along on her seat. Yolanda had to turn her head to hide her smile. She wondered why anyone would come into the berry fields in short pants.

"Have you finished that box already?" Kim seemed surprised when Yolanda replaced the filled box with an empty one from the crate. "My, you pick fast. Maybe your row's better than mine."

"No *diferencia*. You no can stop to talk. Just pick, pick, pick."

Kim nodded. For the next few minutes she picked doggedly, saying nothing.

"Who is your friend?" whispered Rosie from the row beyond.

"Her name is Kim. She seems pretty nice."

Rosie looked doubtful, and Yolanda smiled at her reassuringly. She wouldn't forget. The friendship of gringos had to be proved; it didn't do to take up with them too soon.

On the next row, Albert and Roberto were talking with the girl behind Kim. She was a large girl with a booming voice, and at the same time she chatted with the boys, she appeared to be carrying on a conversation with some of the pickers on distant rows. Her name, Yolanda gathered, was Kelly, and shouts and remarks for Kelly came from the lengths of the rows assigned to gringos. Yolanda told herself that it would be nice to be as popular as Kelly. Everyone wanted to talk with her and share their jokes with her.

She got up and carried her box back to the crate. Two more, and it would be filled. Ninety cents worth. Eighty, really, since she would have to give Juan Sanchez a dime.

"I'm trying to keep up with you," confessed Kim. "I'm getting better, too. See, I've filled one box and part of another."

"You do fine," Yolanda told her. "I have more practice."

"I know," agreed Kim. "I probably shouldn't even try to keep up with a migrant. I just wanted to see if I could."

Yolanda tried to put down the funny feeling she always got when she heard the word "migrant." There was nothing wrong with it. It was a perfectly good word and meant someone who traveled. Traveling was what they did when there were harvests to be gathered. Still there was something in the way people said "migrant" that wasn't nice. It was the way they might say "dirty" or "stupid" or "inferior." Yolanda knew she wasn't dirty, and she didn't think she was stupid. According to the Constitution of the United States, which they had studied in school, she couldn't be inferior either, for it said all men were created equal.

She was so busy thinking of these things that the dirt clod took her by surprise. It came flying through the air and hit her in the small of the back.

"You guys!" yelled Kim. She stood up, facing the rows behind her. "You stop that. You didn't come anywhere near Kelly. You hit Yolanda. Stop it, or I'll call Mrs. Pepper."

Mrs. Pepper, the large lady with the whistle, did not wait to be called. She came puffing up the row, her face flushed with anger.

"Now I warned you about that. No dirt clods! Kim, I'm surprised at you."

"I didn't throw it, Mrs. Pepper," protested Kim. "Somebody over there's throwing them. They're trying to hit Kelly."

"Then Kelly has been returning them," declared Mrs. Pepper angrily. "Because they're coming from here, too."

"It wasn't me, Mrs. Pepper. I can't throw that far," denied Kelly promptly. "It's these two boys next to me. These migrants."

"You say we should throw," cried Albert indignantly. "We no throw nothing till you tell us."

Mr. Truaxe appeared from the end of the row. He looked very serious, and Yolanda's heart turned over. The owners were very grand people, rich and powerful. She wondered what he would do to Albert and Roberto.

"The migrants are here to work," said Mr. Truaxe. "They depend on their earnings for their livelihood. They haven't time to play around, not unless someone stirs them up. You mean these two boys here?"

Mrs. Pepper nodded, and Yolanda saw that her flushed face was turning a shade redder.

"Suppose you two boys go over and pick along with your folks," suggested Mr. Truaxe. He didn't seem to be angry with Albert and Roberto after all. "Somebody can come back and do this row later on." He looked at Yolanda and Rosita. "I guess we can leave you two where you are. You don't look like the kind to throw dirt clods."

In mid-morning most of the gringo children took a rest period. They had brought candy bars and

43

cokes, and they ate them now. Yolanda's stomach was growling, but when Kim offered her half a candy bar, she refused. She didn't want to be in debt to a gringo, even a nice one. She kept on picking. There were three crates punched off on her ticket, and she was nearly through the fourth. The day was going to be hot, and the best picking was in the morning.

At noon the people from Tierra Agreste rested for half an hour while they ate strawberries and the cold tortillas they had brought with them. At the field they could have all the berries they wanted, although the practice of carrying produce back to camp was frowned upon.

Tomas and a few of the older boys got into an argument with some of the gringos at this time. Tomas would not repeat what the boys had said, but it might have turned into a fight if Mr. Truaxe had not stopped it. Yolanda knew the remark had been something bad about migrants. It always was.

At the end of thirty minutes, the Mexican-Americans returned to the fields, but the gringos took a full hour. It was getting very hot. The sun beat down on their bent backs, and perspiration streamed from every pore. Yolanda tied a cloth around her forehead to keep the water from running into her eyes.

By twos and threes, the gringo children straggled back into the fields, but most of them did not stay long. They soon returned to the shade at the end of the rows. It was almost as hot there, but at least they could lie stretched out, drinking tepid water or coke.

Shortly before two o'clock, Kim came back down the row where Yolanda was working. Her plaid shirt clung to her wet back and her face, arms, and legs were burned a fiery red.

"We're going home, Yolanda," she announced. "Mrs. Pepper says it must be 102 degrees. She's afraid somebody might have a sunstroke, and then all the parents will blame her because she's platoon leader. I wanted to say good-by."

"It is hot," agreed Yolanda. She sat back on her heels and smiled up at the girl who had tried to be her friend.

"Of course, it's different with you," said Kim. "You don't feel it the way we do on account of your skin. Mrs. Pepper says that's why dark-skinned people always work in the fields. They don't feel the heat."

Yolanda stared up at her in amazement. Not feel the heat! How ignorant could people be? Of course she felt the heat. She was every bit as uncomfortable as Kim, but she wasn't working to buy a camera that developed pictures in sixty seconds. She was working in the sun so the Ruiz family could eat next winter. It had always been that way. Dark-skinned people worked in the sun because they had to, not because they liked it.

"Well, I've got to go," said Kim. "The bus is tak-

45

ing us back to town. It was nice meeting you. If it's cooler tomorrow, we'll be back, and I hope you're still here."

Yolanda forced herself to smile. She knew that Kim had tried to be nice. It was too bad she had spoiled everything by repeating an ignorant remark.

"We will be here," she said politely.

But when they returned to camp, there was some question about their being there the next day. Nailed to the door of every cabin was a large printed card that read "Condemned."

4

"THE SIGN DOES NOT MEAN that you must leave,"
explained Juan Sanchez. "Some snooper from
the Bureau of Labor was out here today. He put up
those notices. But that is all he can do, only nail
them on the doors. He cannot enforce them. En-
forcement is the duty of the county sanitation officer, and he may not get around to doing anything
for weeks. Pretend they are not there."

Yolanda stared at him scornfully. The *bandido*
Sanchez was probably up to his favorite trick, fool-
ing the people. As long as he got his ten cents a crate,
he didn't care whether or not they got in trouble.
Perhaps she was the only one who suspected. She
and Tomas, who had not trusted Sanchez from the
beginning.

"This bureau—this officer you speak of—it is
government?" asked Señor Corona fearfully.

"Certainly, he is government. And he will be

back," said Pablo Galindez. Yolanda looked at him gratefully. Perhaps she and Tomas would find an ally in their distrust of the *bandido*.

The people of Tierra Agreste murmured in alarm. Government was something they did not understand, and most of them did not care to. It was better to stay far away from government, to keep out of government's sight. That way one might be forgotten.

"It would be better to go on tonight," suggested Señor Matta. "Juan Sanchez, you already tell it is no more than sixty miles to the raspberries, and the trucks are ready."

"You will lose your bonus," cried Sanchez quickly. "I had not told you before, but Mr. Truaxe pays a bonus to those who stay out the season. And the raspberries are not ready. You would sit and wait as you did for the celery."

"Better to do that than to go against the government," declared Papa firmly, and everyone agreed.

As she helped her mother prepare a hasty meal and gather up their belongings, Yolanda told herself that she was glad they were moving on. Señor Sanchez wanted them to stay, and that was reason enough to go. But there was another reason, too. Tomorrow the gringo children would be back.

Although she had been lucky in meeting Kim, Roberto had said that Kelly was not so nice. She had asked a great many questions about what they had to eat, their home in New Mexico, and their personal lives. They had answered politely, but she had laughed at everything they told her and had passed many of the answers on to the others, who seemed to find them amusing also. The boys had been relieved when Mr. Truaxe sent them to pick on their parents' rows.

It was just as Yolanda and Rosie had already agreed. Gringo children were to be avoided, like the government.

As she washed the supper dishes, she amused herself with planning a fitting punishment for the one who had laughed at Albert and Roberto. She imagined Kelly sitting on one of the benches in the Plaza at home during the Easter fiesta. All the children of Tierra Agreste were there, having their annual fun. This time it was Kelly who was the outsider. She was the only gringo. One by one the children cracked their raw eggs on Kelly's unsuspecting head, then everyone stood back and laughed. With yellow yolk streaming down her face, Kelly wouldn't think Mexican-Americans were so funny. And since she was alone, with no one to complain to and nowhere to go, she would see how it felt to be in the minority. Just imagining it made Yolanda feel much better.

It had been four o'clock when they came in from the fields, and it was after six when they drove out of camp. Two Indian families had ignored the no-

tices. Yolanda could see the women bending over
the stoves, their faces lighted by the flames as they
turned the fried bread they were preparing. The
Indian children stood and watched the trucks pull
away, and one little girl raised her hand and waved.

"Her name is Carrie," explained Maria, as she
waved back. "She is nice. I asked her why they
stayed, and she said they had no place else to go."

"I am glad we do," said Rosie, "Juan Sanchez is

a burro, but he knows where all the camps are."

Yolanda did not answer. She hated to give the *bandido* Sanchez even this much credit.

There was a four-lane highway all the way. It by-passed cities and took them straight to the farm-lands in the west. When they reached the outskirts of a small town, Juan Sanchez signalled the second truck to wait while he went inside a store and spoke with someone on the telephone. When he returned, he was smiling.

"It is all arranged," he told them. "Your cabins are waiting. Even Mother Nature smiles upon you. The hot weather is bringing on the raspberries faster than they expected. Picking will start in a few days. Follow me, if you please."

"Do you know what I am going to do when I get there?" asked Yolanda, as Señor Matta started up the engine. "Stand under our very own shower for a solid hour! When I am really clean, if Mamacita has not already done it, I will put all our clothes in the washing machine."

"She will do that herself," Rosie assured her. "My mother talks of nothing else. She has the dirty clothes all ready to go in the machines when we arrive."

Juan Sanchez led the way out of town over a narrow winding road. By now it was growing dusk, but the people of Tierra Agreste sang as they rode along. They forgot that they had worked a long day in the fields and were tired. They were arriving at their new home, a home for three months, which was as long as they sometimes wintered in New Mexico. Only this one promised to be fine and comfortable with certain luxuries they had never known.

At last they drove off the road and into a field. It was flat and treeless. There was little grass, and what had survived grew in thin yellow wisps, well coated with the dust from cars and trucks. Facing them were row after row of one-story, flat-roofed houses, all painted a hideous shade of pink. They were identical, with small windows and a front door reached by a single step.

Mouths dropped open in surprise and disappointment as the people staggered from the trucks. These were not the cabins so gloriously described in the posters in the Plaza; these were not the summer homes, approaching luxury, which Juan Sanchez had promised. This was just another migrant camp. They had seen hundreds like it before.

Yolanda was one of the first on the ground. After one horrified glance at the rows of ugly pink cabins, her eyes searched for her elder brother. Probably Tomas had suspected this from the beginning. He must have reasoned that a man who was a thief would be a liar, too. She had been stupid not to think of such a thing herself, but she had wanted so much for the cabins to be the way they were described.

If Tomas found any satisfaction in being right, he didn't show it. He stood with the others, his face expressionless, saying nothing. Yolanda knew she must do the same. What she wanted to do was to jump up and down with rage, to shout that Juan Sanchez was a thief and a liar, but she couldn't. Nice Mexican-American girls did not behave that way.

"They may be better inside," whispered Rosie hopefully.

Yolanda shook her head. "I see a water faucet.

Farther down is another. And there are the garbage cans."

She had known just where to look. One outside water faucet for every four or five cabins. An equal number of garbage cans, which would be emptied twice a week, if they were lucky.

A man had come from behind a row of cabins, and now he and Juan Sanchez were shaking hands. He was a gringo and was introduced as Mr. Rice, the camp supervisor.

"I'm glad you folks came early," he told them. "Berries are ripening faster than we figured on. These two rows of cabins along here are empty. I thought you'd like to be together, so I've been holding on to them."

"*¿Donde estan las maquinas por lavar las ropas?*" asked Señora Corona.

"Where are the washing machines?" Pablo Galindez translated for his mother-in-law. "Señor Sanchez say they will be here."

Yolanda held her breath. This, too, was undoubtedly a lie. But Mr. Rice surprised her.

"Sure we got washers." He smiled proudly. "A couple of them, both automatic. We got a company to put them in for us this year. It's a concession. We just furnish space. They're only two bits a load. The drier runs a little more, ten cents for ten minutes, but the hot water's free. You'll find the laundry just off the women's shower room. It's down that way.

The men's shower is over to your left."

When they understood, the women exchanged rueful glances. They had thought the washers would be free. Still, they assured each other, twenty-five cents a load was not a great deal to pay, not when there was money coming in each day.

They had misunderstood about the showers, too. From what Juan Sanchez had told them, they had thought that private showers with hot and cold water were in each cabin. There were always stories of the ideal camp that had such luxuries. People would not tell the stories if they were not so. Always, though, it was the friend of a friend of a distant cousin who had stayed at such a place, and the exact location had been lost in the retelling. This camp was like the others—community shower rooms with flushing toilets, one for the men, the other for the women. These were required by law, and lack of them was one reason the Truaxe camp had been condemned.

"Where is the house of the doctor?" asked Pablo Galindez. "My wife will need his help in a short time."

"You'll have to go into town for a doctor. None out here," said Mr. Rice.

"But the posters! They say free medical attention," insisted Pablo.

"And free dentists," added Papa.

Mr. Rice looked embarrassed.

"I reckon the person that made up those posters got a little carried away," he admitted. "But in town you can go to the county health service. You'll get free doctors and dentists there. The government pays for it."

"We do not look for charity. We pay our way," declared Papa scornfully. He turned away, and one by one the people of Tierra Agreste followed his example.

The cabins were clean and smelled of disinfectant. Yolanda looked around with the feeling that she must have been here before. Everything was familiar —the standards set down by law. The single room was regulation size, eight feet by twelve. There were two double beds, nailed to the wall, with springs and mattresses. There was a gas plate for cooking, and a charge would be made for the gas used from the tank of butane which stood outside the window. There were four straight chairs pushed against a wooden table, and an old fashioned ice box, which Mama would use for storage, since there would be no nearby place to buy ice. Above it some shelves were nailed to the wall. Two sliding screens for windows lay on top of the table.

"So," said Mama briskly. "We are here. Yolanda, help me make up the beds. Tomas, you and Roberto unpack the food and dishes. Stack them on the table. I will put them away later."

Yolanda looked at her mother, wondering how

she could accept the disappointment so calmly. They
had expected so much, and it was just as it had always
been. They would be hot and squeezed together,
breathing dust or sloshing through mud, depending
on the weather, yet Mamacita managed to smile.

"I will tell you what we will do," said Mama,
when she had straightened the last blanket. "We will
go to the shower room, you and Maria and I. I will
put our dirty clothes into the washing machine and
let it work for me. You and Maria can get clean with
hot water and soap."

It was what she had wanted to do, and Yolanda's
spirits lifted a little. Even though it wasn't their own
private shower, the hot water would feel good.

Mama had accumulated quite a pile of clothing to
be washed. Since they had no basket, the three of
them carried the shirts and pants and towels in their
arms.

The alleyway between the rows of cabins was deserted, but it was not dark. Almost every door had
been left open, and light from the single bulb,
which hung on a cord in the center of each room,
streamed out into the night. It was as though they
were walking through a checkerboard of light and
dark. They could hear the voices of the people inside. Some were still complaining; others had accepted the situation and were speaking of other matters.

The shower and laundry building was on the end

of the row of cabins. It was painted in the same shade of pink.

"We are the first," said Maria in surprise, for there were no noises of running water or voices from within.

Yolanda agreed it was strange. Rosie had said her mother was anxious to get to the machines, and she was sure the others would be, too. They were lucky to be ahead of the crowd.

They entered through a hall, and to the right was the laundry; the toilets and showers were straight ahead.

"Ah!" cried Mama in delight. She turned off the hall and into the laundry.

There were two glistening automatic washers, with round glass windows and many knobs on top. Beside them was an automatic drier, and a long table for folding clothes. There was also a machine that said, "Soap 35¢."

"I cannot read the directions, Yolanda," confessed her mother. "You must read them to me."

"It will do no good to read them to you tonight, Mamacita." Yolanda's eyes were on another sign, prominently displayed, which said, "These machines may not be operated before 6 a.m. or after 8 p.m."

"It gives very little time." Mama's forehead wrinkled thoughtfully when Yolanda read her the sign. "We must be in the fields at six, and it is five by the time we are back. This is a large camp, with many people, and only two washing machines."

"Come look at the showers," urged Yolanda. "Since you cannot wash tonight, you can have a shower. It will make you feel good."

But no one had a shower that night. When they went down the short hallway, there was another sign. It read, "These showers must not be operated before 6 a.m. or after 8 p.m."

5

RASPBERRY PICKING BEGAN three days after their arrival, and almost at once their lives settled into the routine Yolanda knew so well. They were up at four, and loaded into the trucks that would take them to the fields by five. En route they made two stops, the first to leave the toddlers at the Migrant Day Center in the basement of one of the town's churches, the second to deliver the six-to-nine-year-olds at North Plains School. In these two matters, the *bandido* Sanchez had not lied, Yolanda conceded grimly. The smaller children were taken care of without charge.

She always looked longingly at the school building in the morning and again when they stopped in the late afternoon. How fine it would be to attend a school like that! There were so many windows that the rooms must be as light as out-of-doors. In such a school she could surely pass into the fifth grade very quickly. But she was twelve, and twelve was old enough to work.

One evening, soon after their arrival, notices were posted in the shower rooms requesting all the people to gather in the empty field behind the cabins. This was strange. It could not be the gringo owner who summoned them. He would give orders to the field bosses or the camp supervisor, who would relay them to the heads of families.

When they arrived, they were surprised to find a stranger, a Mexican-American like themselves. He was short with broad shoulders and a smiling face. But for all his good manners and gentle voice, Yolanda decided she would not like to have him for an enemy. He looked determined, like one who was used to giving orders and having them obeyed. He said his name was Martin Garcia, and that he was director of the Valley Migrant League.

The people from Tierra Agreste had never heard of such a thing, but some of the others in the camp who had traveled more widely nodded with understanding. It was a fine organization, they said loudly, it did much good for the workers.

"Is it like the organization of Señor Chavez?" whispered Yolanda. "Will it make strikes, so we cannot work?"

Rosie shook her head. She didn't know either.

Señor Garcia must have realized what some of them were thinking, for he hurried to explain. The

Valley Migrant League did not sponsor strikes. It worked in a small way to improve conditions in camp and among the workers. The Migrant Day Center was due to its efforts, also the summer school.

Yolanda looked at him with respect. She wished the Valley Migrant League would do something for twelve-year-olds who didn't want to fall behind in school.

League inspectors would come regularly into each of the many camps, continued Señor Garcia. If they found one dirty, they had the authority to force an owner to clean it up. If a worker was mistreated in any way, or lied to, or taken advantage of and the fact was reported to the League, Señor Garcia would help to right the wrong. If necessary, a lawyer would be found to take the case to court.

"*¡Esta atarantado!* He is dizzy!" whispered Rosie sneeringly, but most of the listeners were grimly silent.

Yolanda knew that Señor Garcia had lost ground, and she was sorry. Anyone who had helped the younger children go to school should be smarter than that. Surely he must know that the courts were only for rich gringos and that the verdicts were always in their favor.

If he knew, he gave no sign but went right on speaking. Once a week, someone would bring a screen and a projector into camp, and movies would be shown. There was nothing to pay. The movies would be free.

Some of the tenseness left his listeners, and a few of the boys shouted "*Olé.*" This was a real service, and they were grateful. There was nothing to do on summer evenings before bedtime. The meeting broke up on a happy note. Everyone had decided to overlook Señor Garcia's great mistake in assuming that the law was for Mexican-Americans, too. He was a good man, a friend, for bringing them relief from monotony with his moving pictures.

When the last berry had been picked, the cucumbers were not ready, so there was a wait before they could go into the fields. Again there was nothing coming in, and the parents were grateful that children in summer school were provided with free breakfasts and lunches. Two meals a day saved on the grocery bills.

Many of the nine-year-olds who had previously helped with the harvest now entered school for the first time, and it was decided that both Roberto and Albert should go.

"Roberto is ten, and he gets to go," said Yolanda resentfully, as she watched her brother put on a clean shirt and his tennis shoes. "I should go, too."

"This school is for those who are six to nine. Ten is only one more than nine." Mama pulled Roberto closer, inspecting his ears for dirt. "You are twelve. They would send you home."

"But I will never get into the fifth grade. When

we get home, the teacher will say I have not finished all the work in the fourth. She will make me start again, the way she did last year."

"Perhaps this year there will be a new teacher, and she will pass you on, as they did Tomas," said her mother consolingly. "It happens so."

Yolanda knew she was right. It was the custom. When students grew too old or large for one class, they were passed on to the next one. But that wasn't what she wanted. It was foolish to study the same things over and over, things you already knew, when there was so much more to be learned.

"Walk with me and Roberto and wait with us for the truck," suggested Maria. "You have nothing else to do."

"I might as well," agreed Yolanda unhappily.

The crowd of children waiting by the road was large and noisy. Those who were attending for the first time talked of little else but the breakfast that would be awaiting them at school. They were all hungry; they had not shared in the family meal since they would be eating so soon.

"What will we eat?" Roberto grasped Maria's arm, peering down into her face. "What is going to be for breakfast?"

"Eggs. Toast, lots of toast. Or pancakes. Cereal. Fruit. It is different on different days, and you can go back for more if you are still hungry."

Yolanda had eaten two tortillas, but she found

64

her mouth watering at Maria's words. How fine it would be to have a different breakfast each day—not always the same thing!

"The truck will be crowded," said Maria. "There are twice as many going to school today. The teacher will be surprised to have so many new children."

When it finally arrived, the truck was already half filled. It had stopped at other camps before coming to theirs. It was not the same one that usually picked them up, and the driver was a stranger.

"Hurry up and get in," he yelled, leaning down from his seat. "I'm behind schedule."

"Good-by." Yolanda gave Maria a little push. "Study hard."

Laughing and shouting, the children climbed into the back of the truck, leaving her there alone. She told herself that jealousy was a sin, that she should be glad Maria, Roberto, and the others were going to school. It did no good. She wanted to go, too.

Suddenly she was aware that the driver was still leaning from the truck. This time he was shouting just at her.

"What's the matter with you? Get in! You're holding up the works."

"But—"

"Get in," he roared. "Don't make me get out and throw you in. You kids ought to realize it's a privilege to be educated. We're not running this school for fun. It's to learn you something. Now get in this truck and no back talk!"

His face had grown very red, and he glared at her angrily. Yolanda moistened her lips. He was a gringo, and gringos did not like it when you didn't do as they said. Without a word she climbed up into the truck.

All the children had witnessed the scene, and the truck buzzed with speculation. No one blamed Yolanda for obeying the driver. He had ordered her into the truck and had given her no chance to explain. But what should she do now? A big girl of twelve wasn't allowed in the school to which they were going. What would they do to her when she arrived?

"You can go to my room with me," offered Maria. "My teacher is nice."

Everyone protested that was the worst possible solution. Maria's class was for seven-year-olds, and Yolanda would be noticed immediately.

"You will have to go with us," said Roberto finally. "You can say you are nine and big for your age. There will be so many new children today that they will not look too closely."

Yolanda agreed that was the best solution.

North Plains School was in the country, several miles out of town, but near many of the crops they were here to harvest. Yolanda remembered the large windows and thought how lucky she was to see inside the rooms. She thought of the green lawns surrounding the school, so unlike the dusty grass around the camp. From a distance it had looked as thick and cool as moss, and now she could actually touch it. How good it would feel to take off her shoes and run . . .

Shoes! For the first time since she had climbed in the truck, she was aware that she was barefooted. They all went that way in camp to save wear on expensive shoes. She looked around, examining feet. Everyone else was wearing something—sandals, slippers, tennis shoes. Only she was without.

"I cannot go in," she whispered to Maria. "I have no shoes."

"But you have to have shoes!" declared Maria loudly.

Everyone heard, and everyone was concerned. Of course, Yolanda must have shoes. They were required in school. Her old faded blouse and skirt were acceptable, but bare feet were not.

"As soon as they show us our room, you sit down. Fast," said Roberto firmly, when it became apparent there was no solution to this problem. "Keep your feet under you. Maybe no one will notice."

"All out," shouted the driver loudly. "What are you waiting for? I'll be back here at four o'clock. Don't anybody be loitering around. When you see the truck, pile in. I don't wait for stragglers."

The children got out and advanced toward the

school. Roberto and Albert organized the nine-year-olds, who were attending for the first time, and they walked in a tight group with Yolanda in the middle. She was taller than any of them, but at least her feet were hidden.

A young woman with brown wavy hair and smiling eyes stood at the front door when they entered. She nodded and spoke to each child, calling many of them by name. As the little group of nine-year-olds arrived, her smile was even wider.

"We were expecting extra children today," she told them. "We heard that the cucumbers weren't ready. I hope you'll be with us as long as you can. Your room is number four. *Nombre quatro.* It's straight down that hall. Go right in. Mrs. Grayson is waiting for you."

Mrs. Grayson, who was to be their teacher, was friendly, too. She was short and plump and not in the least confused to find that her class of three had suddenly grown to twenty-seven.

"Sit any place you please," she told them. "The bell will ring in a moment, then we'll all march in to breakfast. When we come back, I'll take your names and we'll get started."

There were no desks in the classroom, only chairs. But there were tables, and Yolanda sat in front of one, holding her feet close together and being careful not to squirm or move around.

She had a second moment of alarm when the bell

rang and Mrs. Grayson told them to form a single
line to march in to breakfast. She obeyed quickly
and was relieved that the teacher seemed too busy to
notice anyone's feet. There were other lines in the
wide hallway, adding confusion, and again Yolanda
breathed freely. Everyone was looking ahead, not
down.

Breakfast was every bit as splendid as Maria had
claimed. The line passed before a long counter
where the food was displayed. First they were given
trays with silverware wrapped in a paper napkin;
then they were invited to choose from an assortment

of dry cereals. There were sugar bowls and cream pitchers, and no one said, "That's enough," before they had taken as much as they wanted. There were dishes of stewed fruit to choose from—peaches or figs—and a nice lady in a white cap heaped hot scrambled eggs onto a plate and added buttered toast, with a dab of jelly on the side. Finally, there were paper cartons of milk with straws to drink it through.

Yolanda's eyes grew rounder and her smile wider as she watched the food accumulate on her tray. She forgot about her bare feet, and when she saw that Roberto and the other nine-year-olds had carried their trays to a table on the far side of the room, she hurried after them.

On the way she passed a group of teachers, including the one who had greeted them at the door. They were eating their breakfasts, and they all looked up as she passed. The one from the door smiled, and Yolanda smiled back before she hurried on to join her brother.

In her enjoyment of the meal, she did not remember her bare feet until she returned to the classroom. She hurried back to the table, hoping that the teacher would let her stay there until lunch. So far, Mrs. Grayson had not seemed to notice that Yolanda alone was without shoes. She had not even mentioned her extra height. It was probably because she was too busy, going from one student to another, asking names and writing them down on paper.

At last she came to Yolanda.

"Your name?"

"Yolanda Ruiz." She said it slowly so Mrs. Grayson would understand the pronunciation.

"You are from one of the camps, Yolanda?"

"Yes, ma'am."

"And you are nine?"

"And some months." It wasn't right to tell a lie, not to this teacher who seemed so nice. She hoped Mrs. Grayson wouldn't ask how many months past nine.

Mrs. Grayson didn't ask, but she smiled. There was something in the smile that told Yolanda the teacher had guessed her secret.

"Please let me stay," she begged. "Please no send me back."

"I hope you can stay, Yolanda," said Mrs. Grayson sympathetically. "And so does Miss Andrews, the principal. I'm afraid you'll have to go see her. There are rules, and we have to obey them."

"I will wear shoes *mañana*," Yolanda promised. "I no know today I come."

Mrs. Grayson looked down. Perhaps she hadn't even noticed the bare feet, not until they were called to her attention. When she looked back at Yolanda, her smile was very gentle.

"Go see Miss Andrews," she repeated. "Her office is the first door to the left. She's expecting you."

6

MISS ANDREWS PROVED to be the lady who had
greeted them at the front door. She sat behind a desk in a room that was larger than the whole
cabin in camp. Sunshine poured through the two
huge windows, and it was just as Yolanda had imagined. The room was as light as out of doors. There
were flowers in a vase and a case filled with books on
the wall behind the desk. Yolanda sat in a chair
across from the principal and pulled her bare feet as
far beneath her as possible.

"Your name is Yolanda Ruiz," began Miss Andrews. "How old are you, Yolanda?"

It was no use. They wouldn't let her stay.

"I have twelve years."

"You are small for twelve," said Miss Andrews,
smiling. "But there are rules, and they must be observed. Why did you come today? I'm sure it
wasn't just for the free meals."

"Oh, no," objected Yolanda quickly. "It was mistake. The driver he no would listen."

She went on to explain how the driver had mistaken her for one of the students and insisted that she get in the truck. He drove too fast for anyone to get out en route, and when they arrived, there was nothing to do but come in with the others.

"I will have a few things to say to that driver," declared Miss Andrews sternly. "It is his fault, not yours at all. Perhaps a little later, when I have a few things cleared away, I can drive you back to your camp."

"Please let me stay," Yolanda pleaded. "I no will eat the food again. In the fourth grade they study maybe things I no have learned."

"You are in the fourth grade?" asked Miss Andrews. Her voice was even and without surprise, but Yolanda knew that she must be making an effort to keep it that way. Who wouldn't be surprised that a twelve-year-old was not in the fifth grade?

"For three years," she reported sadly.

Miss Andrews understood immediately.

"You always leave before the term is over. And when you return, they hold you back."

Yolanda nodded gratefully. She wished Miss Andrews were the teacher in Tierra Agreste. Perhaps things would be different.

"Every night I pray to Our Lady," she admitted sadly. "I ask her to pass me to the fifth grade, but there are prayers more important for her to answer."

For a moment the principal sat thoughtfully, then she turned and selected a book from the case behind her.

"This is a fourth grade reader," she said, opening it in the middle and handing it across the desk. "Suppose you read for me."

It was a strange book, not the one they used at home, but it was not difficult. Yolanda read it easily. When she finished, Miss Andrews took a fifth grade book from the shelf. Yolanda read that, too.

"You read very well," said Miss Andrews approvingly. "Of course, there are other subjects covered in the fourth grade, such as math and science and social studies."

Yolanda nodded unhappily.

"The ability to read well is more than half the battle. Many people have been self-educated. They taught themselves by reading books." Miss Andrews replaced the reader and selected several other volumes from the shelf. "Regulations do not allow me to let you enroll in school, Yolanda, but there is nothing that says you cannot help out in the office. You can run errands and sharpen pencils, and when Miss Curtis, my secretary, is away from her desk, you might answer the telephone. When you're not busy, I suggest that you study these. Answer the questions at the end of each chapter. Start in the math book where you left off in school. Read everything in the text and study the examples. If you have trouble, Miss Curtis or I will be glad to help you." As Yolanda began to smile, she added quickly. "I'm afraid that I won't be able to pay you a salary. But you will be given your breakfast and lunch."

A salary! Who cared about a salary? Not when there was a chance that she might pass into the fifth grade next fall! If only the cucumbers would hold off, just long enough for her to read everything in the three books on Miss Andrews' desk. Then she remembered that she was here to help out. She must work for this privilege, and the reading must be sandwiched in between her other tasks.

"I work hard," she promised. "I do everything you say. What do you want that I make first?"

"Why don't you relieve Miss Curtis at the desk in the outer room? I have some dictating, and you can greet anyone who comes in. Ask their names, then come and tell me. You won't have to bother about the phones. Miss Curtis can take the calls in here."

Yolanda jumped up, then stared down at her feet in dismay.

"I embarrass you," she said miserably. "I no have shoes."

"Lesson number one. 'I don't have shoes.' Or 'I have no shoes.' It's not, 'I no have shoes,' " said Miss Andrews, but she smiled when she said it. "A second language is hard. When I make mistakes in Spanish, I hope you will correct me, too."

Yolanda smiled back. It was the same correction the teachers in Tierra Agreste were always making, but this time there was no sting. She was not made to feel, as she usually did, that she was stupid and inferior. All the children talked this way, and it was easier to say than the stilted wording in the lesson books. But if Miss Andrews wanted her to change, she would. It was small payment for the privilege of attending school.

Miss Andrews got up, crossed the room and opened a door. When she switched on the light, Yolanda could see that it led to a tiny cubbyhole of a room, with a bar reaching from one wall to the other. There was a shelf above, on which were stacked a few boxes and sacks. A raincoat hung from the bar and also a sweater, and there were hangers for other garments.

Miss Andrews bent down, and when she straightened up, there was a pair of beautiful blue leather slippers in her hand.

"Try these on," she suggested. "We can stuff cotton in the toes. I always keep a pair of bedroom slippers here. Sometimes my feet get tired by the end of the day."

They were large, but Yolanda declined the cotton in the toes. By shuffling a little, she could keep them on her feet. They were the most beautiful shoes she had ever worn, soft and pliable and of a color that must have been taken from a summer sky.

"Why don't you take the books with you?" asked Miss Andrews, when Yolanda prepared to relieve Miss Curtis at the front desk.

"I work now," Yolanda told her firmly. "I no read the books—" She paused, her face flushing as she groped for words.

"I won't read the books," prompted Miss Andrews encouragingly.

"I won't read the books only when I no—don't have work to do." The sentence came slowly, but it came.

Miss Andrews smiled and nodded. She called Miss Curtis into the inner office, and Yolanda proudly took the secretary's seat behind the desk.

There were no visitors that day. One of the teachers came to the office, but she did not ask to be announced. She went straight to a row of pigeon holes and took out a paper.

"I see we have a new secretary," she said.

Yolanda smiled proudly. She hoped the teacher would glance down and notice the blue slippers, but she didn't. When one was sitting down, slippers were not so noticeable. She wished she had a proper dress to go with them. It would be blue, with a skirt so full that it twirled when she walked, and a sash with a big bow. She would wear flowers in her hair—the blue bachelor buttons that grew in the fields around here would be just right. She pretended that she was wearing the blue dress while she sat at the desk.

The phone rang several times, but Miss Curtis answered; and a child delivered a note for Miss Andrews, which Yolanda carried to the door of the inner office. The dictation took quite awhile, and she began to wish that she had brought one of the books with her. It was a waste to sit doing nothing.

Finally, she picked up a newspaper on the desk and began to read the large print. She had never read a newspaper, and before long she discovered that the big words were the titles of the stories printed below. Sometimes the words were long and unfamiliar, but by reading the whole sentence, she found that she could often guess the meaning.

The stories were all mixed up on the same page. She read about a speech made by the President of the United States; about a plane accident that had killed several people; about a war that seemed to be going on in some country she had never heard of; and a small story reporting that the state had been without rain for thirty-eight days, but the weatherman said a storm might blow in from the ocean and give relief.

She was so engrossed that she did not even hear Miss Curtis return, and she jumped guiltily when the secretary spoke.

"Do you enjoy the paper, Yolanda?"

"*Lo siento mucho*. I am sorry." She hurried to her feet, almost losing the blue slippers. Her cheeks flamed scarlet. "It was there. I no mean to do anything wrong."

"But you didn't," the secretary assured her. "I'd finished with it, anyway. Take it with you when you go home. There's lots more to a newspaper than the front page. Maybe your folks will enjoy it."

When Yolanda climbed into the truck at four o'clock, she carried not only the newspaper, but also the three books Miss Andrews had lent her. The books she would read at home and bring back tomorrow, but the paper did not have to be returned. Miss Curtis kept insisting that her parents would enjoy it, and Yolanda didn't want to tell her that neither of them could read or write.

Mama had not been worried at her absence, for someone from the camp had seen Yolanda get on the truck with the other children. It had been reported to her immediately, and at first she was very angry. She had told Yolanda that she was too old to go to school, and it seemed that she had deliberately disobeyed.

Roberto and Maria came to Yolanda's defense, and when Mama heard how the driver had issued orders and refused to listen, her anger disappeared. Gringos often behaved in this manner. They did not care to hear explanations from a Mexican-American.

When Yolanda told her about Miss Andrews and how she said that Yolanda might finish the fourth grade by herself, she looked doubtful.

"She is a grand lady, and it is kind of her to help.

But the cucumbers will be ready in a few days. When that happens, you will be needed in the fields."

"But I may go every day till then?" begged Yolanda.

"You may go each day till then." Mama smiled at her affectionately. "But do not expect a miracle. The señorita is not the Virgin of Guadalupe."

It was the night for movies in camp, but Yolanda did not go. She sat in the cabin below the single light bulb, reading her books. As soon as she finished a chapter, she asked herself the questions at the end. When she did not know the answer, she went back and read the passage again, memorizing it carefully. She worked the page of arithmetic problems on paper provided by Miss Andrews and carefully folded it away. The principal had promised to check it the next morning.

Since there would be no picking on the following day, the people stayed up later than usual. They lingered on after the film, discussing what they had seen. Then they began returning to the cabins.

"Close the light," said Papa firmly. "We cannot sleep with the light on."

Yolanda's eyes were smarting from staring at the black type, but she shut the book reluctantly. There was so much to learn and so short a time. She had only until the cucumbers were ready, and while she wasted those hours in sleep the cucumbers would continue ripening.

7

IT WAS A NIGHT the people from Tierra Agreste would talk about for years to come.

Shortly after midnight, Yolanda was awakened by a pounding on the door and a frantic voice calling for her mother.

"Señora Ruiz! Please come! My mother asks that you come."

"Who is it?" There was a stir in the darkness, and Yolanda heard her mother's voice from the next bed.

"Pablo Galindez. Please hurry, Señora. It is Antonia. She is going to have our baby, and Grandmother Corona says there is something wrong."

"At once," called Mama quickly. "Tell your mother that I am coming."

The overhead light was turned on, and Mama began dressing hurriedly. Yolanda watched her through heavy eyes. Poor Antonia, she thought. All during the raspberries, she had seemed better. She had picked every day with the rest of them, even managing to stoop awkwardly for berries that grew low. She had seemed to lose some of her fear and had made a joke of her fat stomach and clumsiness. And now that the time was here for the baby to arrive, things were not going well.

Papa got out of bed and reached for his clothes.

"There is nothing you can do," Mama reminded him. "This is women's work."

"I should be with Manuel Corona," he insisted. "Manuel will remember that he signed with Sanchez because we were promised a doctor. He will want friends with him now."

"Very well." She wound the long braid about her head, secured it with pins, and snatched up an empty water bucket and the newspaper Yolanda had brought from school. "I am glad to have this," she said. "Thick papers are useful in times of sickness and when a baby is being born."

"Stay with your brother and sister," Papa told Yolanda, as he followed Mama out the door. "This is not a time for children."

Yolanda looked at Maria and Lennie, who shared her bed. Neither had awakened, but they had both turned in their sleep, away from the overhead light bulb. For a moment she considered getting up and returning to her books. After all, her parents had gone, leaving the light burning. Then she decided against it. Her eyes still stung from the reading she had done that day. She got up and turned it off.

When she awoke again, her parents were coming through the door. She could see them quite clearly, for there was daylight behind them and light was creeping through the small windows of the cabin.

"Was it a boy or a girl?" Yolanda sat up in bed, forgetting about Maria and Lennie.

"We do not know." Her mother's voice was tired, and the circles beneath her eyes were dark. "They have taken Antonia away in an ambulance. She will have the baby in a hospital. We could not help her."

"A hospital? An ambulance?" Such a thing had never happened to someone from Tierra Agreste before. Yolanda could hardly believe it.

"Froban Oro, one of the workers from Texas, offered to drive to town in his car for a doctor," explained Mama. "First he went to the office of the Migrant League, but they were closed. There was a sign on the door that gave the address of Señor Garcia, and Señor Oro went there. When he explained about Antonia, Señor Garcia found a doctor who was willing to come and called an ambulance. They took Antonia away."

"Will she be all right?" asked Yolanda fearfully.

"Only God and Our Lady know." Mama sat down in one of the chairs, as though she could no longer stand on her feet.

"This League of Señor Garcia," said Yolanda's father thoughtfully. "It is of some use after all. Some of the young men were talking. They think we should tell the señor of the lies told us by Juan Sanchez. He asks that we speak of wrongs that are done us. They think it would please him if we trust him with our confidence." He shook his head. "But it would come to nothing," he added.

When the truck called for the children that morning, Yolanda carried the three books and the completed math paper. The problems had been difficult, and yesterday she had worried that she had not done them right. She did not think of that this morning. She was more concerned for Antonia, who had been taken away to a hospital in an ambulance.

"Did your parents enjoy the newspaper?" asked Miss Curtis, when she reported to the office.

"Oh, yes." Yolanda remembered the satisfaction with which her mother had tucked it under her arm before leaving for the Galindez cabin. "Mama was happy for it. We thank you."

"That's wonderful." Miss Curtis beamed with delight. "You must remember to take it home every day. I've always finished reading it by the end of school."

Miss Andrews was pleased that Yolanda had finished a chapter in each book and answered all the questions. She found mistakes in several arithmetic problems, but she was not angry. She explained them carefully and Yolanda listened, promising to try harder.

"You are doing very well." Miss Andrews patted the thin shoulder under the bright yellow sleeve. "And you look very pretty today, like a fresh dandelion in a green field. You will be a decoration to the office when you relieve Miss Curtis."

Yolanda smiled proudly. She was glad that her mother had agreed that she could wear her best dress to school today. It was almost new, less than a year old. They had bought the material last fall at the end of the harvest when there was money. Mama had made a yellow dress for Yolanda and a pink one for Maria, and they had been worn only to church and fiestas. Already Yolanda's was getting short and tight across her chest. Perhaps they could buy material for another in November; then this one could be for school.

The day raced by. She was so busy with her studies that she almost forgot about Antonia. Her chores were very few, so she had plenty of time to read the school books. She had dusted Miss Andrews' desk when she arrived and sharpened all the pencils. She relieved Miss Curtis twice and read the front page of the newspaper while she sat at the desk.

Once she walked down to the gym and delivered a note to the teacher in charge. It was the period when Maria's class was there, and the seven-year-olds were playing Farmer in the Dell. Yolanda was surprised to hear them sing the familiar words in Spanish. She thought Spanish was forbidden in school, but even the teacher, who was one of the circle, sang of the *perro,* the *gato* and the *ratón.*

"It's raining," said Miss Curtis, when the bell rang for dismissal at four o'clock. "You'd better open the newspaper and hold it over your head. Your mother can dry it out before she reads it."

The children shouted with delight as they came outside. The past weeks had been hot; the little cabins were stuffy and uncomfortable; and there was no shade in the camps. The rain, which came down in huge, wet drops, cooling the air, was welcome.

Yolanda remembered the story she had read in the newspaper about the approaching storm. The people who foretold this must be very wise. She had her own reason for rejoicing in the rain. It might hold back the ripening cucumbers, and she could stay in school longer.

Rosie and Concha Matta, another twelve-year-old, were waiting for the truck when it reached camp. They had found a little protection from the wind by standing close to Martin Garcia's parked car, but it could not shield them from the rain, which dropped from their rebozos in steady streams.

"We are to go to your house," called Rosie, as soon as Yolanda jumped to the ground. "All the mothers are at mine. They do not wish us to hear what they say."

"It is about Antonia," guessed Yolanda quickly. "Has the baby arrived?"

"A boy." Rosie nodded. "I am an aunt. No one knows when he and Tonia can come home. They say she is very sick. The doctor told Pablo she could not have had the baby here. She would have died, and the baby too."

Yolanda's hand traced a cross in the rain. It was not unheard of, of course—sometimes both mother and baby died at birth. That it had nearly happened to Antonia was very frightening.

"The baby is in something named the incubator," said Concha. "He came before his time."

Rosie glared at her angrily.

"You had no right to tell her. Tonia is my sister, and the baby is my nephew. I was going to tell that."

Concha flushed and looked down at the muddy field. Yolanda felt a little sorry for her. Concha was a nice girl, but her spine was like a blade of grass. She couldn't stand up for herself. She was always grateful when Rosie and Yolanda included her, but if they made it clear they didn't want her around, she would go away, patiently waiting for the next time.

"What difference does it make who told me?" Yolanda's tone was a little sharper than usual. "Everybody knows the baby is early, and I do not know what that thing called incubator is."

Concha looked at her gratefully, and Rosie seemed surprised.

"The toilets are stopped up again." She added the second piece of news before Concha had a chance.

"And all the new garbage cans have big holes. The garbage is leaking all over."

Yolanda frowned. Someone was always stopping up the plumbing and destroying garbage cans as a gesture of disapproval. This time it must be to show resentment because there was no doctor in camp, after they had been promised one. Of course, it would cost the owner money to set things right, but Yolanda wished there were another way to show displeasure. It worked a hardship on those in camp while they were waiting for repairs.

"My books are getting wet," she said shortly. "I am going inside."

"As you will," agreed Rosie. "Concha, you need not come if you would rather go back home. The Mattas' house is full of *niños*," she explained to Yolanda. "All the Mamas at my house sent them over there to play."

Concha turned to go, but Yolanda saw the disappointment on her face.

"Wait, Concha," she said impulsively. She didn't know why she was angry with her best friend. They had excluded Concha before, but suddenly it didn't seem right to use her this way. "You cannot come to my house, Rosie," she said severely. "I need to study my lessons."

"Study your lessons?" Rosie's astonishment showed on her rain-washed face. "What for?"

"I want to be in the fifth grade next year."

"Perhaps we all will." Rosie shrugged. "It depends on who is the teacher. They may pass us all on, and then this work of yours will be for nothing. Right, Concha?"

Concha smiled faintly but did not answer. Her eyes were on the paper-wrapped bundle in Yolanda's arms.

"These are books," explained Yolanda proudly. "If I read them all, I can be in the fifth grade, and you two will still be in the fourth."

"Burro!" said Rosie rudely. "Come on, Conchita. It is more fun at your house, anyway."

When Yolanda opened the cabin door, she realized she would not have the privacy she had expected. Tomas was there, sitting at the table under the dangling light bulb, knotting a rawhide belt.

"I must study my lessons," she told him defensively.

He glanced up briefly, then looked back at his work without speaking. Tomas was in another of his moods, Yolanda thought resentfully. He was getting worse all the time. Only a year ago they had been good friends. She could talk to him then, tell him things that she was embarrassed to tell other people. Sometimes Tomas even made up little stories—the way she did—about things that couldn't possibly happen. But lately he didn't want to talk to anyone. He had even stopped making those comments that infuriated Papa. But Yolanda could tell by the way he looked that he was still thinking them.

She unwrapped the books, thankful for the thick newspaper that had kept them dry. Then she slipped out of her best dress and put on her old one, setting her soggy tennis shoes in the corner out of the way.

"Where is Lennie?" she asked.

"At the Mattas'. So are Maria and Roberto. I told them to go there when they got home from school. Mama is with the Coronas, and Papa and the old men talk at the Rojos'. Señor Garcia is there, too." It was a longer speech than she expected, and Yolanda was encouraged.

"Are they going to tell him about Juan Sanchez and the lies he told us?" she asked eagerly.

"Certainly not." His voice was scornful. "They are afraid."

"But last night Papa said there was talk. He said some of them thought Señor Garcia ought to be told."

"They will not tell. If he wishes to find out anything, he must ask the right person." Tomas frowned, and Yolanda knew that he didn't want to talk any more.

She opened one of the books and sat on the bed, trying to read. The words didn't make sense. Her mind was too busy with other things. She thought of Antonia and the baby who had almost died; of how mean she and Rosie always were to poor Concha; and that she and Rosie had had a real quarrel. Rosie wouldn't forget that in a hurry, either. She thought of Martin Garcia talking with the older men like her father, who could tell so much about the *bandido* Sanchez if they would. Only Tomas said they wouldn't.

From time to time she tried to concentrate on the book, but the words didn't mean anything. Finally she got up and crossed the room, listening to the rain pounding on the low roof. It sounded as though it would never stop, and she put her nose against the streaming window to look outside.

A man was walking between the rows of cabins, headed for the parking place. His collar was pulled up around his ears, and his hat was low on his head. Nevertheless, she recognized the director of the Valley Migrant League. Martin Garcia's talk was at an end. He was going home, and all the sins of the *bandido* Sanchez were still untold.

It was a single step to the door, and she threw it open with a bang. Dimly she heard Tomas call out in surprise, but she did not stop. Mud squished between her bare toes as she ran, and the rain pounded on her bare head.

"Señor Garcia," she called wildly. "Señor! Please stop. Please come in. We have much to tell you."

Señor Garcia halted, peering out from under the dripping brim of his hat. The next moment Yolanda had reached his side. She clutched his arm and began pulling him toward the cabin.

"What is it?" he cried in alarm. "What is wrong?" But he came, and that was what mattered.

Tomas was standing in the doorway. On his face was a curious expression, a blending of astonishment and alarm. He stepped back to let them through.

Yolanda did not stop until she had pulled Señor Garcia inside and closed the door.

"So, Tomas," she ordered. "He is here. You said he had not asked the right person. You tell him. Tell him all about Juan Sanchez and how he lied to us and cheated us. Tell him, Tomas. You are the right person to tell this."

"You have lost your senses, Yolanda," said Tomas stiffly. "I have nothing to tell. I am not a man. I am fourteen years old, as Papa is so quick to remind me."

Martin Garcia took off his hat and shook the rain from it. He looked first at Yolanda, then at Tomas, and smiled.

"I have already heard much about Juan Sanchez," he said gently. "But I will be glad to hear more. What is it that you can tell me?"

"You have heard something?" asked Tomas cautiously. "Papa and his friends have told you?"

"Very little." Garcia's tone was rueful. "I have been questioning them, but they do not wish to be involved. Some of the younger men speak more freely. Pablo Galindez, whose wife was taken to the hospital, has signed a complaint. We cannot have crooked labor contractors fleecing our people. Nor can we have growers who lend themselves to false claims. They give the legitimate contractors and growers a bad name."

"What will you do?" asked Yolanda. She couldn't help feeling disappointed that Tomas was not the one to expose the *bandido*. After all, he had been the first to suspect.

"Will we get our money back?" demanded Tomas quickly.

"I hope so. Eventually. It will be for the court to decide. I have obtained a good lawyer for Pablo, so we have a chance."

Yolanda swallowed hard. She had never thought it would come to courts and lawyers. Now she was glad that Tomas had not been the one to speak out.

"There is a good chance that Pablo will win." Señor Garcia seemed to read their thoughts. "Juan Sanchez is Mexican-American, too. The judge must choose between them. Pablo has plenty of witnesses, even though we do not have a copy of the poster."

Tomas began to grin. He held up one finger, a signal for them to wait. Then he fumbled under the bed until he found the shoe box that contained his special treasures. No one else was allowed to touch the box, and when he opened it, he turned his back so they could not see what it contained. A moment later he held out a folded paper.

"I do not know why I saved it," he admitted. "But when I saw how carefully Sanchez was collecting all the posters he had put up, I took one. I did not think they were worth anything. I was just being mean."

"You were being smart," declared Martin Garcia.

He unfolded the limp sheet and began to read aloud in Spanish all those fine promises Juan Sanchez had not fulfilled.

8

AFTERWARDS YOLANDA could not imagine what had made her dash into the rain and drag Martin Garcia into their cabin. She had done it without thinking. Well-brought up Mexican-American girls did not do such things. They were quiet and polite; they were never bold and forward. They did not run up to strangers and fill their ears with complaints and accusations.

She blushed with shame every time she remembered what she had done, but she was glad, too. If she hadn't behaved in such a way, Señor Garcia would not have had the poster; Tomas would never have known it was important; and it would have stayed hidden in the shoe box. It was too bad that Tomas would not get credit for contributing such an important piece of evidence, but Garcia seemed to think it was best.

"I will not say where I got the poster," he had told them. "I am afraid your father would not like you to be involved. He wishes to have no part in this himself, and I would not have him blame you in any way."

Tomas had understood and agreed. Papa would be very angry—there was no telling what he might do. Tomas would be happier if he did not find out. He hoped no one had been looking out a window at the moment Yolanda ran into the yard.

Yolanda hoped so too. For days she worried about it, but the angels must have been watching over her. They had kept the people from looking out their windows at that moment.

By the next morning everyone in camp knew what Pablo had done, and by evening the news had spread to the other camps. The names of Juan Sanchez and Pablo Galindez became familiar to everyone, and people talked of nothing else. Opinion was divided as to whether Pablo had been right in taking action against the labor contractor. Generally the arguments were between the younger men of Pablo's age and their fathers. The young men shouted, "Sue!" while their elders advised caution.

Yolanda paid little attention to the arguments. She was too busy with her studies.

On Sunday she decided it was time to make up the quarrel with Rosie. Her eyes were tired from all the reading she had done the day before, and besides Papa had brought disquieting news to the cabin the night before.

The young men—the Chicanos, as they called themselves—were planning to hold a parade. Papa did not say what kind of parade, but he did not approve. He said it was a bad thing, and would lead to trouble for all of them. From the way Tomas listened, without lifting his eyes from his plate, Yolanda could tell that he disagreed with Papa, but he wouldn't say anything. The only person who could tell her about the parade was Rosie. Rosie made it her business to learn everything that was going on.

It was early morning when she stepped out of the cabin. The camp was barely astir after a late Saturday night, but she saw her friends immediately. Rosie and Concha were sitting on the Mattas' front step, staring at the Ruiz cabin. It was almost as though they had been expecting her.

As soon as they saw her, they both looked away, and when she came up and spoke to them, Rosie pretended to be surprised.

"Why, it is Yolanda Ruiz. I wonder why she is not studying her lessons. Why is she wasting her time on us, Concha?"

It was easy to tell that Rosie was still upset. She hadn't calmed down in the past few days, as Yolanda had hoped. Instead, she must have been letting the resentment build up inside her.

"This is Sunday," she explained mildly. "I studied all day yesterday. Now I come to see my friends."

"What a favor you do us," said Rosie coldly. "Is it not good of Yolanda to bother with us, Concha, when she is so busy with important things?"

Concha didn't answer. She looked down at her bare toes, which were tracing little circles in the thick dust.

"I have to do my studying first before I can do other things." Yolanda was determined not to get angry. No matter what Rosie said, she would keep her temper. "If I do not get my lessons, I cannot pass into the fifth grade."

Rosie laughed and jabbed Concha with her elbow. It was a signal to share her own disdain for such an ambition, but Concha did not laugh. She continued tracing circles with her toes.

"What is new?" Yolanda's voice was a little grim. Rosie was being unusually difficult.

"What do you care?" asked Rosie. But the temptation to be first with the latest gossip was too strong. She had to continue. "My brother-in-law, Pablo Galindez, is a hero. Today all the young men from every camp in the valley will honor him. Some of our people who live in town and never go up the road any more will honor him also. They will have a parade."

"My father said there was talk of a parade," said Yolanda cautiously. She mustn't say too much. It would please Rosie to be the first with the news. "He did not say what kind, but he does not like it."

"Neither does my father," admitted Concha, looking up from her circles. "None of the older men do."

"The parade is to proclaim our rights," said Rosie. She began waving her hands, as though she were making a speech. "The gringos forget that we have rights, but we are Americans, too. Mexican-Americans. The idea for the parade came from some of the people who live here, but it was the brave actions of my brother-in-law that gave them courage."

"I still do not understand," admitted Yolanda. "What kind of parade? Will there be bands? And floats with pretty girls riding on them?"

"It is not that kind of parade. It will be marchers only; they will wear arm bands and carry signs. The signs will tell of the bad things that have been done to us."

"Like not having a doctor here when we were promised one?"

Rosie nodded, and Concha added, "Our men are making signs about that. They will be about all the lies that were told us before we came. Someone saved one of the posters Señor Sanchez put up in the Plaza. We have proof."

"There will also be signs of other wrongs," said

Rosie quickly. "The people who live here say there is discrimination. The rents are too high, and they are even higher for Mexican-Americans. Our people cannot get good jobs. Those all go to the greedy gringos."

"Tell her about the owner and his gun," said Concha.

"There is a camp near here, and the owner will not let any outsiders visit." Rosie smiled, pleased that Concha had deferred to her. "Not even the people from the Valley Migrant League. When Señor Garcia tried to enter, the owner barred his way. He fired a gun in the air and said that the next time he would take aim. The Chicanos from that camp will have signs telling of that."

"Just think, those poor people cannot have any movies," said Concha softly. "Perhaps our camp is not so bad after all."

Yolanda shook her head in amazement. She could hardly believe that all these things had happened in the past few days. She had been so engrossed in her school work that she had missed all the talk. Papa would not permit such discussions in his house, but surely some of the children must have repeated parts of it in the truck. Then she realized that she never paid much attention to their conversations. They were all younger, and usually they spoke of silly things that were not worth hearing.

"Will the parade do any good?" she asked. "Will it right these wrongs?"

"Who knows?" Rosie shrugged her shoulders. "The Chicanos think it will. They say it is the thing to do—to have a protest march. At least everyone will know we are here."

"They say the police will be there, too," said Concha in a small voice. "They will have guns."

"But they will not use them. Not if we march peacefully and cause no damage," insisted Rosie. "At the head of the parade will be my brother-in-law, Pablo Galindez."

"It is too bad that Tonia is still in the hospital and cannot see him," said Yolanda. "It is a great moment for your family."

"Tonia would be very proud," agreed Rosie. She smiled brightly, and Yolanda knew she was forgiven. Rosie's anger might linger a long while, but with the proper overtures it could vanish swiftly.

The parade was not scheduled until afternoon, but when they drove in to Mass, they could see that some of the citizens were getting ready. Several store windows were protected with sheets of plywood, and men were putting white painted trestles that said "No Parking" along the main street.

"They think we will make trouble," mumbled Tomas, eying these precautions scornfully. "We Chicanos do not plan violence. We are going to have a peaceful march."

Yolanda, who was sitting next to him in the back of Señor Matta's truck, was alarmed.

"What do you mean 'we Chicanos'?" she whispered. "You are not going to march?"

"If I can get away from Papa, I am," he insisted, then refused to discuss the subject further.

As usual, the women prepared a meal after they returned to camp, but only the younger children had appetites. The Chicanos went immediately to the field behind the cabins. They were too excited to think of food, and the older people were too nervous. Although they had heard of protest marches, this was their first experience with one.

As soon as they had eaten, all the children gathered behind the last row of cabins where they could watch the departure of the Chicanos.

"I wish we could be in the parade," said Rosie wistfully. "But ladies do not march in parades, not unless they are religious or for a fiesta."

"Sometimes they do," objected Yolanda. "The secretary at my school gives me her newspapers. Sometimes it has pictures of ladies marching in parades."

"Not nice ladies," protested Concha quickly.

"The paper did not say, but they looked nice. Besides, there was Joan of Arc. Remember when our teacher told us about her last year? She was a lady, and she even led the army into battle. I think they made her saint after her enemies burned her."

Rosie claimed that she had never heard of Joan of Arc, but Concha remembered. While she was refreshing Rosie's memory, Yolanda let herself imagine how it would feel to be a modern Joan of Arc.

She saw herself at the head of all the young Chicanos, marching through the streets. She was wearing her yellow dress, the one Miss Andrews said made her look like a fresh dandelion, and her hair was unbraided and hanging down her back. When the gringos saw her—a young girl—at the head of the band of protesters, all thoughts of violence faded from their minds. The policemen threw down their guns; the gringos bowed their heads in shame that they had not realized the many injustices before. Everything changed overnight. There were fine jobs for those who wished to stay here; all the camps showed movies every night; and each cabin had its private shower and was enlarged to three times its present size. All because of her, Yolanda Ruiz.

"You have that funny look on your face again." Rosie's voice jerked her back to reality. "What are you thinking about?"

"Just the parade," Yolanda admitted quickly. "I hope there will be no trouble."

"They are starting now!" cried Concha. "Look!"

The Chicanos were grouping themselves into a

line of march. They were six abreast, with two of their number as parade marshals to keep them in formation. Rosie was quick to point out that one of the marshals was her brother-in-law. There were many signs, carried aloft on poles, and although they were too far away to read, Yolanda knew what they would say. They would proclaim to the world the lies that had lured the people of Tierra Agreste to this particular camp.

There were, perhaps, forty or fifty protesters marching across the dusty field, and Yolanda's eyes went up and down the lines anxiously. Tomas was not there. At first she was relieved, and then she knew that it was too soon. Doubtless her brother planned to join their ranks farther along the line, when he was safe from Papa's eyes.

"They cannot go! We cannot let them go. Perhaps it is to their death!" cried a woman's voice close by. "There could be men with rifles on the roof tops."

For the first time, Yolanda noticed that the older people had come out of the cabins and were standing with the children beside the field. Her eyes sought for and found Papa, then Mama, but Tomas was not there.

"We cannot stop them. They are grown men." That was Concha's father, Señor Matta. He had a younger brother with the marchers, and his voice was grim.

By now the Chicanos had reached the edge of the field. They turned and started down the graveled road that led to town. The sunlight picked out the white cardboard signs that bobbed along like white poppies.

"At least I can follow. If harm comes to my Carlos, I will be there," cried a woman, and she hurried after the marchers.

"Wait. Maria, come back," called a man's voice, but when she did not stop, he hurried after her. The next moment a whole group of anxious-faced older people started across the brown field, headed for the road. Their children came running behind.

It had been some of the Texas migrants who had begun the exodus, but before long the people from Tierra Agreste joined them. Señor Matta began it.

"I cannot desert Alejandro," he cried. "What if he should be hurt and left lying in the streets? Who would care for him?" When he started across the field, Señora Matta followed.

"We must protect our own," called someone. "Foolish though they may be, they are ours."

Concha had started after her parents immediately, and Rosie was close behind. Yolanda waited only a moment, but when she saw Papa joining his friends, she went too. Mama remained with Lennie and Maria, and Yolanda could hear her voice calling her to come back. She pretended to be deaf. She had no intention of staying behind.

Where the back road forked, the band of Chicanos paused, and their followers waited, too, not in martial lines but in a great huddle of humanity—older men and women, their weather-beaten faces drawn in lines of deep anxiety, and children, attempting to hold down their exuberance so they would continue to be forgotten by their parents.

After a few moments another band of Chicanos, carrying signs and trailed by an anxious crowd of well-wishers, rounded the curve of the connecting road. These were from another camp, and they joined their forces with the first group. One of them had a guitar, and soon all the Chicanos were singing. The music floated backward on the still, warm air and gave a feeling of fiesta to the parade. The older people did not sing, so the children didn't either. But they would have liked to. It was fun, thought Yolanda, marching down the road with the sun shining on her head. It was a break from the monotony, and she was glad that she had come.

Several times they were joined by other groups as the road was crossed by those leading to other camps, so that by the time they reached the main highway into town, there were several hundred Chicanos and even more followers. Another contingent of equal size awaited them here. They had come from the valley north of town.

But there was something else waiting on the paved highway that made Yolanda's heart rise into her throat—a state policeman on a motorcycle. Her eyes turned immediately to his hip. There it was! A gun in a black leather holster!

The policeman blew his whistle, then raised a bull horn to his mouth so everyone could hear what he had to say.

"I'm here to escort you into town, folks. You've got a permit for a parade, and we aim to see everything's done proper. There won't be any trouble if you don't start it. We've blocked off the highway into town and closed off the streets to traffic. Your permit says you can march down Main Street and circle City Hall. Then if you want to march to the Catholic church, the Father's waiting to say a few words and give you his blessing. After that, you're expected to go home peacefully. No throwing of bottles or bombs. No vandalism. This is a peaceful march."

"That is all we ask," called someone. "A chance to air our grievances."

"Then that's what you're getting." The policeman got on his motorcycle, and the roar of its engine was loud and raucous. "Follow me."

Six abreast, the army of Chicanos marched down the highway into town. Silently, but with less order, their older protectors straggled behind, and the children brought up the rear. The guitar and the singing had stopped. The parade had taken on a somber note. No one knew what was ahead. There could be fighting, perhaps even death for some. The whole thing depended on the gringos who were waiting in the town.

Yolanda wished now that she hadn't come, and she could tell by the faces of the children around her that many of them wished so, too. The excitement had gone out of the day. The policeman had spoiled everything. On the graveled back roads it had been fun, walking with the others in the sunshine, listening to the snatches of song that drifted back. Now she was frightened, and her legs felt stiff and brittle, as though she were walking on sticks. Under the callouses, the pavement burned the soles of her feet.

As they entered the town, she was afraid to look at

the gringos watching on the sidewalk. She knew they were there—she could hear voices—but the words ran together, and she didn't try to pick them out. She kept her eyes on the backs of those ahead, taking one short step after another as she was pushed on by the crowding children behind.

Gradually, she found courage to look from side to side. The walks were jammed with men. There were few women and children. Most of the gringo faces were set and serious, some looked angry, a few seemed sympathetic. Policemen were spaced at intervals to keep order. They made no move toward the guns at their belts, but the guns were there.

Occasionally a voice called out from the crowd, "Go home, if you don't like it here!" Or "Get off the street!" Or "Dirty Mex!" But most of the spectators watched quietly with wary eyes, as though they too were a little frightened.

Yolanda found herself growing angry. They weren't dirty Mex. They were Mexican-Americans, and they kept themselves as clean as possible, cleaner than many gringos. The streets were public property, and the Chicanos had received a permit to hold a parade. They had been invited to this place. They had been begged to come here to harvest the crops. How would the gringos like it if they all walked out and left everything to rot in the fields?

The boarded-up store windows added to her anger. Did the gringos think just because they were migrants they had no respect for property? Did they expect someone to throw a rock and break the glass? And perhaps steal the goods that were on display? They were not thieves. The Mexican-Americans paid for everything they received. Often they had to pay a great deal more than a gringo for the same thing.

No building was more than two stories high, and now she noticed that all the upper windows were occupied. People leaned out, staring down on the marchers below. Her anger dissolved in terror as she looked up. Back in the field the woman had said there might be riflemen on the rooftops. Perhaps some of those people in the windows had rifles, too. How easy it would be to pick off individuals in the crowd! Papa, perhaps, or Tomas—she was sure that Tomas had joined the Chicanos at one of the stops— or any of the people she knew.

She pushed with her hands on those ahead, trying to make them move faster. It had become important to get the march over with and back to the safety of the camp. But the children were crowded together in a tight block and could not be hurried. They moved at the same slow pace as before. The girl next to her was crying, and Yolanda took her hand.

"Do not worry," she said bravely. "Nothing bad will happen. Our Lady will see to that."

The girl squeezed her hand, but she kept crying.

The Chicanos were silent. No one responded to any of the taunts from the sidewalk; they did not even call out their protests. They merely marched, letting their placards speak for them.

There were some men with movie cameras, who were permitted by the police to step into the street and take pictures. Otherwise, the gringos stayed behind the trestles watching. One man, who was very drunk, staggered out and began shouting insults. A policeman took him by the arm and led him away. Yolanda was surprised at that. She had never seen the police side with the Mexican-Americans against a gringo before.

At last, they completed their route and turned into the side street. Ahead was the small Catholic church where they attended Mass, and the Father was standing on the steps. The Chicanos filled the yard around him, spilling out into the street. The older people crowded in at the fringe, while the children were almost a block behind.

She was so far away that Yolanda could not hear what the priest was saying, but when she saw him raise his hands, she bowed her head. She knew he was saying a prayer, and she said her own in gratitude that no one had been hurt.

After that the crowd broke up. The protest march had been conducted safely, and it was time to start the long walk back to camp. Yolanda had become separated from her friends, and she began looking for them.

"Rosie, Concha," she called, hoping she would be heard above all the other voices.

"Yolanda!"

Someone grasped her arm with fingers that felt like wire. She looked up, and there was Papa. His eyes blazed with anger.

"What are you doing here?" he demanded.

9

THE CHICANOS WERE PLEASED with their protest march and claimed it had accomplished everything they intended. Now the gringos realized they were there in force. Had there not been pictures and a story in the newspapers? And the television cameras had been there too. At last their grievances were in the open.

But so far as Yolanda could tell, the march had done little good. It had not changed any conditions, and things went on as they had before. No new jobs opened up for the Mexican-Americans in town; the closed camp remained closed to outsiders; and Pablo Galindez's trial against Juan Sanchez still had not come up in court. Señor Garcia explained that it was now in something called a "docket." That meant there were other cases ahead, and it had to await its turn. Gradually talk about it died away.

Cucumber-picking began, and Yolanda's schooling came to an end. Miss Andrews said she could borrow the books and continue reading the chapters at night, but without help on the math problems Yolanda knew she would never complete the fourth grade. Besides, who could concentrate on lessons after a day of picking cucumbers?

"I wish some bad disease would come along and kill all the cucumbers in the world," she complained to Rosie.

"You are crazy. What would we do between the berries and the beans?" asked Rosie practically.

Yolanda couldn't answer that, but she wished there were another crop to pick. Cucumbers were so hard. The vines grew close to the ground, and the cucumbers seemed to resist the pickers. They clung to the tough stems, and it took a hard yank to get them free. Yolanda crawled and stooped from sun-up until late afternoon, and when it was time to return to camp, she could hardly straighten up. Her bones ached, and she felt as though her joints were grinding together. Even a warm shower was little help. It required a full night's rest to take away the pain, and the next morning in the fields, it began all over again.

She had hoped there would be another break between crops so she could return to school for a few days, but the beans were ready almost before the cucumbers were finished. It was August now, and Yolanda felt that each day seemed to grow hotter. The sky, which should have been as blue as turquoise, was covered with a thin haze.

"Maybe it will rain," suggested Rosie hopefully. "That would cool things off."

"Those are not clouds, but smoke," explained Yolanda. Every day she read the weather story on the front page of the newspaper Maria faithfully brought home from school. "There is a big fire in a forest somewhere."

"It must be close." Rosie stared around apprehensively. "I hope it does not come here and burn us up."

"I do not believe it is close. It is a big fire, and the smoke blows a long way." The newspaper had given the location of the forest fire, but the name meant nothing to her.

"How can it blow anywhere? There is no wind." Rosie emptied her full bucket into the hamper and crouched down to begin again.

Yolanda had to agree with that, but there was no disputing the haze that dimmed the blueness of the sky. It hid the line of mountains in the west and even blurred the cluster of farm buildings on a nearby hill. Her cotton shirt clung to her wet back, and the cloth she had tied around her forehead to keep perspiration from running into her eyes did little good. It ran down anyway.

Like cucumbers, the harvesting of beans was hard

work. It meant crawling, crouching, stooping, walking, but at least she could straighten up occasionally. She wasn't quite so tired at night, and she had been able to read more of her lessons. She was almost through two of the books. Only the arithmetic remained a puzzle.

"I am starting my twelfth hamper," called Rosie. "How many have you picked?"

"Only eight," admitted Yolanda. "Twelve is very good, Rosie. Lots of men cannot pick more than that."

"The good ones can. They pick fifteen or sixteen. Once I heard of a man who picked twenty-four hampers in one day. Someday I will do that, too. I will be the best picker in the whole world."

Yolanda tried to work a little faster, but she knew she could never catch up. Rosie's hands were fast and clever. She was always able to fill her bucket or box more quickly than the others. Probably Rosie would realize her ambition to be the best picker in the world. That would be a fine thing. Everyone would admire her, but Yolanda didn't want that. She just wanted to be in the fifth grade.

When they picked up the school children late that day, there was disturbing news. The summer session was over; it was the last day of school.

"The books!" Yolanda cried in alarm, as Maria squeezed in beside her and handed her the newspaper Miss Curtis had sent. "Miss Andrews' books! If

I had known it was the last day of school, I would have sent them with you

"Miss Curtis says you can drop them by the school anytime," Maria assured her. "The janitor will be there. He has to get things cleaned up for fall."

Supper was ready by the time Yolanda and Maria finished their showers and returned to the cabin. Tonight there was hamburger meat, cooked up with a little chili and rice. There wasn't room at the small table for everyone, so Yolanda carried her plate outside and sat on the single step. She brought Miss Curtis' newspaper with her, hoping to find more about the forest fire which covered the sky with smoke.

The story was on the front page, and it was even longer than usual. The big letters at the top said, "Fire Fighter Killed," and Yolanda began on the smaller print beneath

"A forest fire that has charred 2,800 acres of Southwestern Oregon land claimed a life Wednesday night. Killed instantly by a falling tree was Luis Ruiz, a logger of Trent, Oregon . . ."

"Papa! Papa!" Yolanda did not wait to read any further. Clutching the paper, she hurried into the cabin. "It is Uncle Luis. He has been killed!"

Her father put down his fork and stared at her blankly.

"Luis dead? What nonsense is this?"

"It is here, Papa. It is all in the paper. I only read part of it, but it gives his name and where he lives. It is the same."

"Read it to me." His voice was quiet, and he did not look angry, the way he always did when Uncle Luis' name was mentioned.

Yolanda began at the beginning and read the story to the end. Uncle Luis, with a group of other men, had journeyed from his home to the place where the forest fire was raging. He was working with the others when suddenly a tree had toppled. He had been struck full force by the trunk and hurled fifty feet by the impact. The story went on to tell more of the fire, which continued to burn, and of the efforts to contain it, but it said no more of Uncle Luis.

The little room was very quiet. Everyone looked at Papa, and Papa seemed to be looking far away— perhaps into the past when he and his brother Luis were young and friends.

After a few moments he pushed back his half-filled plate and got to his feet.

"Go on with your meal," he ordered. "I must see Froban Oro. He told me that he wishes to sell his car. I will see how much he asks, and if it is not too much I will buy it."

"Buy it? Buy a car?" Mama's voice was shrill with alarm. "Why would you buy a car?"

"I must go to my brother's home," said Papa

firmly. "We must all go. It is only fitting. Luis and I had our differences, but he always knew that if anything happened to him I would not desert his widow and children. They are our family now. We will leave early in the morning."

10

L OUIE RUIZ?" The man at the gas station stopped
wiping the windshield and came around to
Papa's side of the car. "Sure I know where he lives—
lived. You friends of Louie's?"

"His brother," said Papa.

"Say, I'm sure sorry." His glance included all the
occupants of the old sedan, Papa, Maria, and Mama,
holding Lennie, in the front seat; Tomas, Yolanda
and Roberto in the back. "About the accident, I
mean. The whole town's sorry. It's a terrible thing to
happen. I'm glad you came. Connie will be glad, too,
not that we aren't trying to do what we can to help."

"Thank you." Yolanda did not miss the note of
surprise in Papa's voice. Gringos did not usually
show such concern for the troubles of a Mexican-
American.

"Ed!" He turned to shout, and after a moment a
younger man appeared from inside the service sta-

tion. "You take my car and pilot these folks over to Louie Ruiz' house," he ordered. Then turning back to Papa, "I could tell you how to get there, but this way's easier. You just follow along behind Ed. He'll show you."

"So kind," murmured Mama, when she understood what was taking place.

"That boy is no older than I am," said Tomas, his eyes following Ed enviously. "Look at his fine job! Working with cars!"

For the second time since they left Hillsboro, Papa paid for gas. It was small wonder Froban Oro was so happy to sell his car, thought Yolanda. It ate gas like a hungry man ate tortillas. Still, it had got them here, out of the green valley, over the heavily wooded mountains, and into a land that reminded her of parts of their own New Mexico.

Now the world was largely brown, with great sweeps of dry, desert-like plains below rimrock cliffs. Surprisingly, though, next to the stretches on which only sagebrush and stunted juniper grew were cultivated fields of a green so alive and glowing that they seemed unreal. They were kept fresh by sprays of water from long pipes that traveled slowly through the fields, turning over and over as they went. Even Papa, who was experienced in most crops, could not tell this one by name. It was something he had never harvested.

Tomas read aloud the population of Trent on the

sign at the city limits. It had less than 2,000 people, and the houses sprawled across the brown desert and up the bare slopes to the east. Yolanda observed everything carefully as they drove by. Every house was carefully painted and surrounded by a green yard and flower beds. There were stores and business establishments along the street, and they passed a church and a fine brick school. Uncle Luis had chosen a nice town to live in.

She wondered again about Aunt Constanza, whom she had never seen. All she knew was that Aunt Constanza was a city girl, from East Los Angeles. Uncle Luis had met her at Aunt Minda's house, and they had married and come north to live. That was the whole basis for the family quarrel. Grandfather expected both sons to remain with him and help with the herd of cattle. When Uncle Luis chose to make a life for himself, he was disinherited. Sometimes Yolanda thought it was strange that Aunt Minda was not blamed for living someplace else, but, of course, daughters had to go with their husbands.

As soon as Papa had dug into their winter savings to pay for the gas, they followed Ed's car. After a block he turned, leaving the business district behind. Here the streets were not paved, but they were pounded hard and rolled. The houses were small, with only a few to each block, and the surrounding yards were large, with open brown fields beyond.

Ed pulled up before one of the houses, and Papa

stopped just behind him. He had barely room, for there were other cars parked along the block, some large and new, while one was an old truck.

"This is it." Ed leaned out to speak to them. His eyes were a little curious, but his voice was sympathetic. "This is the Ruiz place. I guess Mrs. Ruiz has company."

"Company?" repeated Tomas softly. "Aunt Constanza has friends?"

The small house was painted white, and a whirling sprinkler kept the neatly cut lawn green. There were beds of scarlet geraniums and white petunias, and a stone duck, followed by a procession of three babies, paraded across one corner of the lawn. It looked very rich and gringo, thought Yolanda. She almost wished they hadn't come.

Papa marched up the walk and boldly knocked on the front door. His family hovered behind him on the steps, and Yolanda could tell by their faces that they shared her feelings. This was not the home of a Mexican-American. They should not be here.

After a moment the door was opened by a tall lady with very yellow hair. She wore blue slacks, with a flowered apron tied about her waist, and for a moment she stared at them in amazement.

"I am Alvaro Ruiz, brother of Luis," announced Papa loudly. "I come to care for my brother's widow and her children."

The lady's astonishment changed to delight. She

held open the screen door, calling over her shoulder.

"Connie! It's your brother-in-law and his family. What a surprise!"

Papa stepped inside, and Mama, holding tightly to Lennie's hand, was at his heels. The others followed so slowly that the lady gave them a gentle push.

"Step in, kids. I want to shut the screen and keep out the flies."

The living room was small and crowded with people. At first glance Yolanda took them all for gringos, then a pretty, dark-haired woman rose from the sofa and stepped forward. This, she was sure, must be Aunt Constanza.

"Alvaro?" She put out her hand a little diffidently, but Papa did not take it. Instead he enveloped her in a great hug, patting her shoulder gently.

When they arrived, Aunt Constanza had been calm. Now she began to cry. She clung to Papa, burying her face in his shoulder.

"Do not cry, little one," said Papa in Spanish. "You are not alone. We are your family. We have come, as Luis would have wished."

The lady who had opened the door took charge.

"I think the rest of us had better leave." Her glance circled the ladies who occupied all the chairs and part of the sofa. "Connie has her family now. She doesn't need us."

The ladies all rose obediently, and the one in blue turned to Mama.

127

"Please tell Connie that if she needs anything to call. We're no farther away than the phone. You'll be staying on till after the services, of course?"

Mama looked confused.

"*No hablo*—no speak," she said with difficulty.

"I will tell," promised Yolanda quickly. "My mother she not understand English."

"Good," agreed the lady. "I'm Mrs. Brown. You'll find my number written down somewhere. Connie won't have room for all of you, but we've got a tent. I'll send it over, and some sleeping bags. You can put it up in the back yard and be quite comfortable."

"Thank you," said Yolanda in amazement.

"There's plenty of food. People have been sending things in all day. You won't have to cook right away," continued Mrs. Brown. "Now be sure to call if Connie needs anything at all. We're all fond of her and Louie. We want to make things easier."

Yolanda nodded, and Mrs. Brown began ushering people out the front door. Each one smiled sympathetically as she left, and as they went by, several ladies patted Lennie and Maria on the head.

By this time Aunt Constanza had stopped crying. She had greeted Mama and met each of the children in turn.

"Such a fine family," she declared. "If only Louie could be here. How happy he would be to see you all!"

"It is my fault," said Papa gruffly. "I am a stubborn man. May God forgive me for my stubbornness. But I will make it up to Luis' widow and his children."

"Where are your children?" Mama voiced the question Yolanda had wanted to ask.

"They're at a neighbor's. I will phone and tell them to come home."

Roberto caught Yolanda's eye, and his eyebrows lifted. Imagine a Mexican-American having a telephone in his house! Even Aunt Minda in East Los Angeles did not have a private phone.

"How many children have you?" asked Tomas eagerly.

"Just two. Debbie is ten and Mark is seven."

Tomas looked disappointed, and Yolanda knew he had hoped for an older cousin, preferably one who owned a car.

"The arrangements for the funeral are all made?" Papa sat down on the sofa and looked about in amazement, at the rug on the floor, the extra chairs, the table which seemed to have no use except to hold a vase of flowers, the electric fan which made a cool breeze across his hot face every time it turned.

"Everything is arranged," she agreed. "It will be at the church tomorrow, with the Rosary tonight. Everyone has been so kind and helpful. I have had nothing to do. And now that Louie's family has come, there is nothing more to ask for."

"You will need money." Papa reached into his

pocket for the purse, which contained their already depleted winter savings. "I have money, and it is yours."

"Oh, no," said Aunt Constanza quickly. "Louie had some insurance. It will take care of everything. Even this house, now that he is gone, will require no more payments. That was in the mortgage contract. At his death, it belongs to me as survivor. And I have my job at the store. Mr. Teal told me to take a few days off, but I will go back to work. We will get along."

"Perhaps you had no need of me," said Papa stiffly. "Perhaps we should have stayed in the fields."

"No, no." Aunt Constanza covered his hard brown hand with hers. "I am grateful that you came. It means a great deal to me. Wherever he is, Louie must know, and he is happy, too. He grieved about the quarrel. He loved you very much."

"As I loved him." Papa leaned back, but he still looked bewildered.

Yolanda knew just how he felt. At great sacrifice, they had left the work that would provide them with food for the winter. They had expected to rescue someone who was all alone, surrounded by un-friendly gringos, to welcome her into their family.

Now they found that the gringos here were not un-friendly, and that although she was bereaved, Aunt Constanza was rich. Just look at the house she owned and its furnishings, the dining room table, glimpsed through the archway, groaning under its load of meats and salads, cakes and pies! Think of the fine job she had mentioned, an inside job that would not require stooping and bending, crouching and crawling, and did not end with the last harvest.

No matter what she said about being glad to see them and grateful that they had come, Yolanda knew that Aunt Constanza could have got along very well without them.

11

I WISH THAT YOU COULD STAY here always," said Debbie. "Mama does too. She says she doesn't know what we'd have done if you hadn't been here."

"We have no—haven't done anything." Yolanda corrected herself quickly. She had tried very hard to make her English like Miss Andrews', and now she was using her cousin as a pattern. It wasn't easy. Debbie spoke very fast. She shortened words: "don't" for "do not," "haven't" for "have not," "I'm" for "I am." But if Yolanda wanted to speak like an Anglo—Debbie said she mustn't say gringo—she must learn to shorten them too.

"It would be lonesome without you," explained Debbie. "And Mama would cry more. Sometimes she cries at night—I hear her. If you weren't here, she might cry in the daytime, too."

Yolanda considered this information carefully. She hadn't known that Aunt Connie cried at night. She had returned to her daily job in the store, but in the mornings and evenings at home, she never cried. At first Debbie's eyes had overflowed whenever she mentioned her father, but these times seemed to be growing less.

"I wish Uncle Alvaro would find a regular job, like Daddy did. Then you could stay," persisted Debbie. "Do you think he could?"

"We have to follow the crops. He don't—doesn't know how to do anything else," Yolanda reminded her. "It was lucky Aunt Connie knew somebody who needed a man for the mint, or we would have gone back to the beans by now."

Debbie didn't answer, but her face puckered thoughtfully.

They were sitting on the front step, watching the twilight creep like advancing gray smoke. The snow-capped mountain in the west that looked by day like an ice cream cone had changed into a gray ghost in a pale sky. The houses farther down the block were hazy bulks. Only the front yard before them was still clear enough to see. It smelled of fresh grass, which Roberto had mowed that afternoon, and the white petunias in the border.

They had been here ten days, longer than Papa had intended to stay. He had meant to see Uncle Luis properly buried, then return to camp, bringing Aunt Connie and her children with them. When he saw that Aunt Connie did not need his financial help or protection, he tried to leave without her, but Aunt Connie did not want to be parted from her new family just as she had found them. If Alvaro needed work, she would find it for him.

She talked one of the farmers into letting him help with the mint harvest, which was the strange green crop they had seen in the fields outside of town. At this stage, the work was all mechanized, but Papa learned to run a swather, a machine that cut the mint and left it for the trucks to pick up.

Mama worked twice a week, cleaning the houses of rich Anglos, but there was nothing for the others to do. This was a great waste, and it made them all uneasy. However, they were careful to keep their feelings from Aunt Connie. It would be discourteous to let her know that she was imposing a hardship upon them. Aunt Connie was a city girl and had never worked in crops. She had just suffered a great tragedy. If having them there a little longer was a comfort, they must make the sacrifice.

"Tell me about your school," Yolanda said at last. "Do you like it?"

"It's all right." Debbie tossed her long, dark hair out of her eyes. It was such pretty hair, and sometimes it was tied with bright ribbons or yarn to match her dresses. Neither she nor her mother wore black to show they mourned the death of Uncle Luis. That was hard to understand, since Mama still wore black for baby Carlos, who had been dead over a

year. Aunt Connie explained that they could not afford to buy all new clothes, but that was no reason.
She had a black dress, and in Tierra Agreste one dress
would be enough. It could be washed when it was
dirty and put back on.

"Is your teacher nice?" persisted Yolanda.

"Miss Parsons was nice. I don't know who I'll get
when I go back. You never do till you get there. The
kids say one of the fifth grade teachers is strict, and
I hope I don't get her."

Yolanda's heart turned enviously. At ten, her
cousin Debbie was going into the fifth grade.

"How about the kids? Are they nice?"

"Most of them. There's a few who are kind of
snobby. They think they're better than anybody else.
But you don't have to pay any attention to them.
There's always somebody around."

"What is snobby?" Her cousin's vocabulary contained many words that Yolanda didn't understand.
It was because Debbie associated with Anglos and
had never learned much Spanish. Mama, who
couldn't talk with her at all, was horrified, and even
Papa was quietly disapproving. Aunt Connie said
that since they would never use it, there was no need
for Debbie or Mark to learn Spanish, and she spoke
to them only in English.

"They're stuck up," explained Debbie. "Their
folks are like that, too. Most of the people here are
nice, but there's a few who think they're society or

something. They don't want their kids to play with the Indians who are bussed in to school from the reservation. They probably don't approve of me, either, but I don't care. There's nothing they can do about it."

"Your school sounds nice," said Yolanda wistfully.

When the mint harvest came to an end, Papa announced that they would leave immediately for the apples. Aunt Connie had written a letter for him to Señor Corona in the Hillsboro camp, asking the name of the orchardist in Hood River who was expecting the people from Tierra Agreste.

Like Papa, Señor Corona was unable to read or write, but the answer came back in Rosie's laborious handwriting giving the name of the new camp. She also added a little news. Pablo Galindez's trial still hadn't come up on the court docket. Since Pablo could not wait around, the judge had deferred it for one year. Pablo would have to come back next summer if he wanted to continue his suit against Juan Sanchez.

Papa shook his head scornfully when he heard that. He had said from the beginning that a Mexican-American could not get justice in a gringo court.

"I wish you would not go," said Aunt Connie. "Our potato harvest starts in October. There will be work in that."

"October is a month away," Papa reminded her. "In a few days it will be September. We must work then, all of us."

"Not the children," reminded Aunt Connie. "School starts in Oregon the day after Labor Day. The law says the children must go to school."

Papa made a bitter face at the gringo law that forced children into school, but he did not argue. Every year the Ruiz children attended many schools —a month here, two weeks there, so short a time in each that they hardly adjusted before they moved on. Even Yolanda agreed it was a waste.

"Why not leave the girls here?" suggested Aunt Connie. "They can start school with Debbie and Mark. They might as well go here as in Hood River. Debbie and Mark and I have talked it over, and we would like to have them. You would be doing me a favor. Yolanda can help tidy up and get dinner started before I get home from work."

Papa hesitated. He looked at Mama, and Yolanda was sure she knew what he was thinking. She and Maria would make two less mouths to feed.

"If they stayed, it might save getting an extra cabin," coaxed Aunt Connie. "Who knows what you will find in Hood River? The cabins may be too small for one family, and it will be too cold for the boys to sleep outside by then."

Papa nodded politely. No one had to be told about the cabins, thought Yolanda. They were all the same size, the minimum required by law. Again Aunt Connie was showing her city upbringing. No one could

137

afford to pay for an extra cabin. They would all squeeze into one somehow.

"Well?" asked Aunt Connie. "May they stay?"

"If you are sure they can be of help," said Papa finally, "If it will comfort you to have your nieces with you longer, I cannot deprive you of them."

Yolanda must have been holding her breath without knowing, for it came out in a great rush. A whole month—perhaps more —all in one school!

"It was my idea," whispered Debbie. "I told Mama it would work."

The next day was Sunday. Mama, Papa, and the three boys left early. As she watched the old sedan drive up the road, trailing a widening ribbon of gray-white smoke from the tail pipe, Yolanda felt a sud-

den pang of guilt. She had suddenly remembered weekends!

Yesterday they had slipped her mind. She had thought only of the saving on the food bill, and the fact that two less in a cabin would be more comfortable. She had supposed Papa was thinking of that, too; now she knew he wasn't. He had agreed to leave her and Maria only because Aunt Connie asked him.

On Saturdays when there was no school, everyone worked in the crops. Sometimes they picked on Sundays, too, when there was danger of spoilage. How much would she have made? How many pounds of beans and corn meal was she depriving her family of by her selfishness? Her eyes filled with tears, and for a moment she considered chasing after the car.

"There, there." Aunt Connie slipped a comforting arm around her shoulder "You mustn't get homesick so soon. They'll be back in a month. And we have lots to do."

"What?" demanded Mark. "What do we have to do, Mama?"

"We have to start making school clothes. You and Debbie have enough to start on, but Yolanda and Maria need lots of things."

"I always have one new dress to start school," Debbie reminded her quickly.

"It won't hurt you to wear an old one," insisted her mother. "Come inside and see what I've been picking up on the remnant table."

Maria was delighted at the prospect of a new dress, and Debbie, who was in on the secret, was anxious to see the contents of the brown sacks her mother had been bringing home and piling on the closet shelf. Mark, who had no interest in clothes, went down the street to find a boy to play with; Yolanda stood quietly, trying to look polite and interested. She would never forgive herself, she thought.

In her mind, she saw her family at home in Tierra Agreste. It was late winter, and the black pot above the fire was filled with boiling water. There was nothing in the water. No beans. No corn meal. The house was empty of food.

"It is all your fault." She could almost hear Roberto's voice sounding in her ears. "If you had only remembered weekends and come with us to pick apples, we would have money to buy food."

"Selfish!" accused Tomas. "Always thinking of yourself."

The others did not say anything, but Lennie and Maria were crying, and she knew it was because they were hungry.

"Which one do you like best?" Debbie yanked on her arm, pulling her thoughts back to Aunt Connie's living room.

"All are pretty." Yolanda blinked as she stared at the four lengths of bright, figured cotton that Aunt Connie had unfolded across the sofa. "But so expensive," she added guiltily.

"Actually, they weren't," said Aunt Connie. "They're remnants—the end of the bolt—so they were marked down. And I had my store discount on top of that. Each one cost less than a dollar."

"You should have got one for me, too, Mama," muttered Debbie.

Aunt Connie ignored her and began opening the last paper bag. It held wool material, one length of red, the other blue.

"I splurged just a little on these," she confessed. "They're remnants, too, but they were two ninety-eight a yard. We can eat hamburger to make up for it. They're for coats. If Alvaro comes back for the potatoes, you'll need them. It gets cold in October. The red is for Maria. There's not so much material in that piece."

In spite of her misery, Yolanda stepped forward and felt the blue cloth that was to be hers. It was soft and warm, the color of shadows caught in canyon walls. She had never owned a coat before. Everyone she knew wore serapes or rebozos in cold weather. She couldn't help being excited about the coat. And she would make it up to her family. When they got home, she'd hardly eat a thing. She'd starve instead of sharing food paid for by the toil of others.

"That's a lot of sewing. Can you get it done in a week?" asked Debbie.

"Not all of it, but at least they'll have new dresses to start school. You'll both need shoes, too," she added. "If you'll meet me after work tomorrow, we'll take care of that."

Yolanda stared at her in amazement. Where was all the money coming from? Of course Aunt Connie was rich, but such expensive presents were beyond her understanding. Two dresses apiece, a coat, and now new shoes! Often children took turns staying home from school so that one pair of shoes could serve several members of a family.

Aunt Connie did not seem to notice her bewilderment. She tugged a sewing machine out of the closet and told Debbie to cover the table with papers so she could spread out the material for cutting.

In the midst of this, the phone rang. After she had talked a moment, Aunt Connie covered the mouthpiece with her hand and turned to Yolanda.

"It's Mrs. Debney in the next block," she explained. "She wonders if you'll baby-sit for her this evening. She says there's a shortage of sitters, and she's at her wit's end to get somebody. She pays fifty cents an hour, and she'll need you from seven until about eleven."

"What would I do?" asked Yolanda blankly. She had never heard of such a thing as baby-sitting.

"Just sit," Debbie explained. "And keep the kids from killing each other. Maybe put them to bed when it's time. Baby-sitting's a snap. I wish people thought that ten was old enough to baby-sit."

"Tell her yes," cried Yolanda eagerly. "I will baby-sit any time she needs me."

Mentally, she counted it up. Seven until eleven was four hours. Two dollars! If she could just find enough babies to sit with, maybe she could make up for the weekends in the apple harvest.

12

THE SCHOOL was a fine brick building with long corridors and many rooms. It reminded Yolanda of the one she had attended so briefly in North Plains. There were a great many Anglo children, hurrying this way and that, calling to their friends and pausing to talk in small groups.

"Where are the Indians?" she asked her cousin anxiously. Debbie had told her that busloads of them were brought here to school. It had been a comforting thought. Indians were a little like Mexican-Americans, but without the Spanish blood. Probably, like herself, they would not be so advanced as the Anglos, and she might not be the only twelve-year-old in the fourth grade.

"Oh, they're all in junior high," Debbie told her carelessly. "They go to the reservation school until seventh grade. Come on. The principal's office is this way. I'll take you there before I go to my room."

The seventh grade! Yolanda could hardly believe she had heard correctly. There was no need for a seventh grade in Tierra Agreste. Sometimes students got as high as the sixth, but generally they dropped out in the fifth.

"Do the Indians want to go to the seventh grade?" she asked, hurrying after her cousin.

"Sure. Even if they didn't, they'd have to. It's the law. You have to go to school until you're sixteen."

That was right. The people who dropped out in the fifth grade always claimed to be sixteen. Tomas was claiming it already.

"What if somebody wanted to go to the seventh grade, but the school didn't have one?"

"Then they'd have to start one," Debbie told her positively. "You can't break the law."

The principal in this school was a man. Debbie introduced him as Mr. Robinson, and he asked Yolanda to come into his office and sit down. There were many interruptions—everyone seemed to need his advice on the first day of school—and she had to wait some time before he was free.

She sat in a straight chair in the inner office, smoothing the striped skirt of her new dress and now and then lifting a foot to admire the fine new oxfords Aunt Connie had selected. She wished Debbie had been allowed to stay; it was a little frightening, waiting all alone.

Finally Mr. Robinson came in and shut the door.

He sat at the desk and began shuffling through the papers on top. When he found the one he wanted, he read it carefully.

"You are Yolanda Ruiz, and you are twelve years old," he said finally. "For a short time this summer you were at North Plains School near Hillsboro?"

"Yes, sir."

"I have a letter from Miss Andrews of that school. She thought you might be attending here this fall and has written us about you."

For a moment Yolanda wondered how Miss Andrews had known she would be here. Then she remembered. In the flurry of departure, she had forgotten to return the books to the school. Aunt Connie had solved the problem by mailing them back, and Yolanda had enclosed a letter, thanking Miss Andrews for her help and explaining the situation. Miss Andrews had not answered, but she had taken the trouble to write to Mr. Robinson instead.

The hard lump in her throat began to dissolve. Miss Andrews was her friend—whatever she had written couldn't be bad.

"She tells me that on your own time you studied all the fourth grade texts and that you completed everything but the math. Is that correct?"

"Yes, sir. I tried to do the problems, too, but they were hard."

"Math is difficult for some people," agreed Mr. Robinson. "However, it is necessary to understand

and complete it as one goes along. Otherwise, one will not be able to do advanced work."

"Yes, sir." Her voice was weak. For a moment she had hoped that Miss Andrews had recommended her for the fifth grade. Now she knew it was impossible. She would have to begin again in the fourth.

"We have a new fourth grade teacher, Miss Sparrow, who is very sympathetic to your problem. She has volunteered to coach you in math during her free period, though it will mean you'll miss the morning recreation hour. Miss Andrews is convinced you can handle the other fifth grade subjects, and she urges us to give you a try."

"You mean I will be in the fifth grade?"

"In everything but math. That you will take by yourself, with Miss Sparrow, until such time as she feels you are capable of joining in the regular class work."

"Oh, thank you. Thank you." The words seemed so inadequate to express what she was feeling. After three long years in the fourth, she was actually going into the fifth grade. She would be in the same class with Debbie, and when they returned to Tierra Agreste, she would be up with Tomas—providing he returned to school. It was all because of Miss Andrews; but Mr. Robinson came in for some of the credit, and the sympathetic Miss Sparrow, who was giving up her free time to make it possible. Yolanda's eyes filled with tears as she thought of all these kind

Anglos. No one had ever been so good to her before.

"Now, now," said Mr. Robinson. "We're just giving you the chance. It's all up to you now."

"Oh, I'll try," promised Yolanda fervently. "You'll see how hard I'll work."

There were thirty students in the fifth grade, and most of them seemed friendly. Yolanda remembered other Anglo schools she had attended for a few weeks and wondered if the friendliness was because she was Debbie's cousin. She decided that part of it was her new clothes. This year she wasn't wearing worn-out tennis shoes and a faded dress that was almost outgrown.

The teacher's name was Mrs. Hogue, and Yolanda was horrified to hear the children call her "Old Lady Hog" behind her back. Mexican-American children were not permitted to speak disrespectfully of their elders, particularly one so educated and grand as a teacher. She was the strict one whom Debbie had hoped she wouldn't get, but Yolanda didn't find her so. Mrs. Hogue demanded that the room be quiet, but that was only courtesy for those who studied. She expected people to know their lessons, but that was why they went to school. She never hit anyone with a ruler or slapped children in the face.

At 10:30, when the others went outside to play, Yolanda went to a special room where Miss Sparrow was waiting. The fourth grade teacher was nice, and she was pretty, too. She had dark hair and eyes, and she wore a red dress with a beaded pendant hanging from a chain. When Yolanda admired the necklace, Miss Sparrow smiled and told her it had been made by a dear friend who was a Cheyenne Indian. Yolanda was glad to hear the teacher had a friend who was an Indian. If she liked Indians, she might like Mexican-Americans, too.

Miss Sparrow had the same book used in North Plains, and she asked Yolanda to show her where she had left off. That was great luck, she told herself. She wouldn't have to begin at the first of the book, as she had always done before. Best of all, Miss Sparrow could explain the problems so they were clear. On the first day, Yolanda worked two pages without a mistake.

"It's too bad you have to spend your Rec Period doing math," sympathized Debbie on their way home from school. "You don't get acquainted with the kids."

"There will be time for that." Yolanda smiled and patted the notebook that contained her next assignment. "I have to catch up so I can do the math you do."

"I don't see why. Half the kids in class can't do it." Debbie sniffed. "Old Robinson's a drag, putting you in a tutoring class during Rec Period."

When they reached home, Yolanda scurried around tidying up. She talked Debbie into scouring the sink, while Mark and Maria ran dust cloths over the furniture. She felt a little selfish because she left the best job of vacuuming for herself. Until they came here, Yolanda had never seen a vacuum cleaner. It was still a marvel, the way it filled with air like a great balloon, then sucked up lint and dirt that were all but invisible until the bag was emptied afterwards.

"Are we having hamburger for dinner again?" asked Debbie, when she had finished her work. "I'm getting sick of it."

Yolanda nodded guiltily. She liked hamburger, even if it was the cheapest kind of meat. Aunt Connie served it often and in many ways—patties, meat loaf, and casseroles—and it never tasted the same. But Yolanda hadn't forgotten that they were making up for the expensive coat material by eating hamburger. No one had mentioned it since the day Aunt Connie had brought out the red and blue wool, but Yolanda wondered how long it would take to pay for that extravagance.

"We're having string beans, too," she told Debbie hastily. "And potatoes and salad and tapioca pudding."

"Ugh," said Debbie, making a face.

Yolanda wondered what she would say to tortillas three times a day, with meat as an occasional luxury.

The weeks sped by. September was almost gone,

and Yolanda was grateful for the warm wool coat. Although the days were bright, mornings and evenings were cold. Sometimes the temperature dipped close to the freezing mark on the thermometer outside the school.

One afternoon Aunt Connie returned from work, and after she had hung up her coat and complimented them on the shining house, she announced that she had news.

"From your father," she told Yolanda and Maria. "Alvaro has sent us a letter. I had better read it to you. Some of the spelling is odd, and it took a little while to figure it out."

She took an envelope from her purse, and Yolanda recognized Rosie's round, painstaking writing on the address.

"Dear Sister, widow of my beloved brother," read Aunt Connie. "I have made up my mind to harvest the potatoes. In the goodness of your heart, please to ask the owner for a job for me and for my good wife, Petra. Also one cabin. Also if you will please to request jobs for my esteemed friend Señor Manuel Corona and his wife, Pilar. Also one cabin at their disposal. Is it still your desire that your nieces, Yolanda and Maria, remain as guests in your home? I am forever in your debt, dear sister. Your brother, Alvaro Ruiz."

"He's coming! Papa's coming for the potatoes, and we get to stay!" cried Maria in excitement.

"You don't have to go home just yet." Debbie grinned at Yolanda triumphantly. "And maybe after the potatoes, we can find something else for Uncle Alvaro to do."

"Wait," said Aunt Connie. "There's a postscript, but I don't think it's from Alvaro. It's in the same writing, but it doesn't sound like him."

"It's from Rosie," explained Yolanda quickly. "She wrote the letter for Papa. What does it say?"

Aunt Connie handed her the sheet of paper to read for herself.

"the burro sanchez ran of we have to get home our selfs your car bust our papas bowt stashun waggun see you soon."

13

WHAT YOU SHOULD DO, Alvaro, is to stabilize, the way Luis did." Aunt Connie leaned across the dinner table, and her voice was serious, as though she had been thinking of the matter for some time. "You ought to settle down in one place and find a full time job."

"My home is New Mexico." Papa looked up from his fried chicken leg, and Yolanda could tell he was making an effort to be polite. Papa didn't like to have women tell him what he should do. "It was my father's home, and his father's, and his father's."

"But you don't own the land any more," said Debbie bluntly.

Papa stared at her first in surprise, then in open anger. He was not used to children who interrupted adult conversations.

"Someday, perhaps, the land will be mine again. El Tigre, who fights for our people, says that is so. He says that someday there will be justice for the Mexican-American, even in the gringo courts." He ignored Debbie and addressed his remarks to Aunt Connie, this time speaking in Spanish.

Yolanda saw Mama stir uneasily in her chair. She had been unable to follow the conversation before, but Mama was always nervous when Papa was upset. She was probably wishing they hadn't accepted this invitation for Sunday dinner.

The station wagon, crowded with the Ruiz and Corona families, had been here for two weeks. Aunt Connie had found jobs for the adults working in the potato harvest, but Yolanda did not see them except on Sundays. The cooperative camp, where they lived, was several miles from town. The children were bussed to school, but it was not the same one she and Debbie attended.

Yolanda had been disappointed about that. She had hoped that Rosie would come to her school, but maybe it wouldn't have worked out anyway.

From the moment the dusty station wagon pulled up in front of Aunt Connie's, she could tell that Rosie had changed. She stared at Yolanda's new clothes, without even saying they were nice. When she was taken on a tour of Aunt Connie's house, she was the only one who did not exclaim over the portable television set, which brought black and white moving pictures into the living room. She had nothing to say about the hot running water in the

kitchen and bath or the electric stove or the toaster that browned a slice of bread, then popped it up the moment it was ready.

All Rosie wanted was to talk about Juan Sanchez and the terrible thing he had done by leaving them stranded. He had sold his fine truck secretly, then disappeared. No one knew where he had gone, but he had managed to take some of the farm workers' money with him. Of course, the police had been notified. They had come to camp and asked many questions, then gone away. That was the last the people of Tierra Agreste expected to hear of the matter.

Since they were left with only Señor Matta's truck, they busied themselves with the problem of transportation. By now they had money from their summer work. It was too bad to spend some of it on cars, but things could have been worse. There was a car lot nearby that offered fine bargains in used automobiles for a few hundred dollars. A car of his own was the ambition of every migrant, and perhaps this was meant to be. Yolanda's father turned in the worn-out sedan as part payment, and he and Señor Corona went together on the purchase of a used station wagon. So far it had proved durable, and they could split the cost of the gas.

Only the Ruiz and Corona families had come to Trent. Most of the people had traveled south to a place called Klamath Falls, which also grew potatoes. Antonia and Pablo Galindez had been among them.

Rosie no longer thought her brother-in-law was a hero. She said he was *atarantado*—silly, confused. How could he have hoped to find justice in a gringo court? Delaying the case for one year was just a trick; and even if it were not, nothing could come of it now that Juan Sanchez had disappeared. But Pablo was stubborn; he said he would go back next year and find out.

While she was telling these things, Rosie had seemed like her old self. Her eyes had sparkled, and she had made little jokes, the way she always did. But when the stories were finished, she grew silent. They could not draw her out, and she was the first one in the station wagon when it was time to go.

Aunt Connie had taken them to visit at the camp the following weekend, and Yolanda had tried again to talk with Rosie. It was no use. She and Debbie had to make all the conversation. Rosie just stood there and after a while, she excused herself, saying she had work to do. Yolanda wondered what was wrong with Rosie to make her act this way.

"Yolanda!" Papa's voice, raised in annoyance, broke into her consciousness. She had been thinking so hard about Rosie that she had almost forgotten where she was. "Your Aunt Constanza spoke to you. Is this the way you behave as a guest in her house?"

"I am sorry," said Yolanda quickly.

"I want you and Debbie to clear the table. We will have our dessert," said Aunt Connie. She spoke

reassuringly to Mama and Papa. "Yolanda is a good girl. She has been a great help to me. She is getting along well in school, and I am sure she has told you about her baby-sitting."

"Yes," agreed Papa. He smiled approvingly, and Yolanda felt a glow of pride. She had been able to turn over $49.75 as a contribution for winter food, and there were more jobs lined up.

The girls cleared the table quickly, then put slices of apple pie before everyone.

"I wish you would think about stabilizing, Alvaro." Aunt Connie returned to the subject that had been so upsetting before. "This is a nice town. Already three Mexican-American families live here. They have found jobs and settled down to raise their families. People treat us well."

"Even if I gave up the land of my fathers, I know nothing but cattle and farming," Papa reminded her. "There is not work in those things in the winter."

"Such jobs are few," admitted Aunt Connie sadly. "You might have to do something else."

Before her family returned to camp, Yolanda had a chance to speak with Tomas alone, and his version of Pablo Galindez's trial was different from Rosie's.

"He has a chance," Tomas insisted stoutly. "Señor Garcia says so. The postponement could have happened to anyone. It was not because Pablo is a Chicano."

"But if Juan Sanchez has disappeared—"

"The owner also is named. He knew that the posters were lies. He did not try to stop them."

"But he is a gringo," protested Yolanda. "Of course the judge will favor him."

"Perhaps not. Señor Garcia told Pablo that it does not always happen. After we left, the owner who would not let outsiders in his camp was forced to admit the Valley Migrant people. The protest march did that. The Chicanos are gaining in power every day, and some of the gringos are not unfeeling. Perhaps they even fear us Chicanos just a little."

"You Chicanos," scoffed Yolanda.

"Yes, us Chicanos," insisted Tomas. "In one more year I will be fifteen. I will look much older then. And I will leave Tierra Agreste to the old men like Papa and go to help others like Pablo Galindez fight for the rights of our people."

"*Tonto!* Dumbbell," said Yolanda derisively, and walked away. Tomas talked big, but she told herself that Papa would never let him do anything silly.

The weeks raced by. Yolanda finished the fourth grade math, and Miss Sparrow began helping her catch up with the work done by the fifth grade since the opening of school.

By now they needed to wear the new coats throughout the day. Even when the sun was bright, there was no warmth. The grass was coated with frost when they started out for school. In the west, Mt. Jefferson and the Three Sisters, towering above the lesser peaks, grew whiter every day as fresh snow fell in the Cascades, and Aunt Connie dug up the geraniums and pulled the petunias out by the roots.

As it grew colder, people talked of nothing but the weather. A hard rain or a heavy freeze would ruin the potatoes, and now the crews worked seven days a week.

One Sunday Aunt Connie borrowed a car, and with the four children drove out to camp. They brought a picnic basket; she thought it would be nice if Mama found dinner ready when she returned from work.

Tomas had found a job picking up the potatoes scattered by the machine, so Roberto and Lennie were alone in the cabin when they arrived. After Aunt Connie's house, the single room looked smaller than ever to Yolanda. For a moment she wondered where everyone would sit when the others returned. Then she laughed at herself for being silly. There would be room for everyone—there always was.

"Did you bring fried chicken, Aunt Constanza?" asked Roberto hopefully, as she began to unload the basket.

"I brought a big pot of chili. And we have salad and garlic bread and a chocolate cake."

"I want some now," demanded Lennie.

"You wait," ordered Roberto sternly. "Mama and

Papa will be here soon."

Yolanda turned on the gas plate and set the chili pan on one burner and the coffee pot on the other. She wondered if she should go over to the Corona's cabin to see Rosie, but she decided against it. Rosie hadn't seemed glad to see her the last time she came.

Mama and Papa arrived with Tomas at their heels. They were grimy from the field, and the dust had settled in lines in her mother's face that Yolanda had never noticed before. Mama looks old, she thought in sudden panic. Lots older than Aunt Connie. It was strange, because there were only a few years difference in their ages.

"Chili!" Papa sniffed appreciatively as he lifted the lid from the pot. "It smells good."

There was not room for everyone at the small table, so Aunt Connie spread out the food and urged everyone to help himself and sit wherever he could find a place. It was crowded but very gay, with everyone laughing and talking at once.

"You make fine chili, Constanza," declared Papa, smacking his lips. "Plenty of meat. Hot with peppers."

"You forget I am Mexican-American, too, Alvaro." Aunt Connie laughed. "It has been a long time since I made chili, though. I cook other things now."

"The years bring changes." Papa's brown face, shining from the soap and water scrubbing, grew solemn, and he put down his spoon. "I have been thinking of what you said, Constanza, that I should leave the land of my fathers. You are right. It holds nothing now for me and less for my children. If I can find a full time job, I will not go up the road again. We will stay here, my family and I We will—what do you call it?—stabilize."

14

"T OMORROW WE MUST START looking for a job for Alvaro," said Aunt Connie, as they drove back to town. "There must be something around here he can do."

Yolanda, huddled in the new blue coat, felt little prickles of excitement run up and down her arms. She still couldn't believe that Papa had agreed to leave Tierra Agreste. Of course, they would all harvest crops in the summer; but to live here during the winter months, to finish school and maybe even go to high school, would be like something out of one of her dreams. Like any dream, it couldn't possibly come true, but it was fun to think about, especially with Aunt Connie and Debbie so convinced that it would happen.

She wondered what Rosie would say when she heard the news. It was odd to think of being parted from Rosie. They had been friends all their lives, but now Rosie didn't seem to want to be friends any more. Perhaps she would be glad if Yolanda did not return to Tierra Agreste.

"You're very quiet, Yolanda," called Aunt Connie from the front seat. She had to speak very loudly to make herself heard over Mark and Maria, who were having a game of counting car lights on the highway. "Aren't you happy about it?"

"Oh, yes," she replied quickly. "I just can't believe it, that's all."

"We're going to have to work hard to find something," said Aunt Connie. "Jobs are scarce. I'm afraid it will take a small miracle."

Yolanda knew whom to ask for miracles. That night for the first time in over a year, she changed her prayers. She did not ask Our Lady to pass her into the fifth grade. Instead she prayed that Papa would find a full time job so they need never go up the road again.

They could hardly wait for Aunt Connie to return from work the next day, but when she came she had nothing encouraging to report.

"I asked all over town. There's nothing. Mr. Bingham was in the store, and I hoped he would have something. He raises fat cattle, and that kind of work is something Alvaro could do well. But Mr. Bingham already has a hired man. He's promised to ask his friends though. Maybe one of them will need somebody."

"Why couldn't Uncle Alvaro be a logger like Daddy?" asked Mark.

"Alvaro is in his forties. It's a little old to start at that." She smiled at them encouragingly. "I've put an ad in the newspaper that will reach the farmers. It will be out on Thursday. I think that's the best way to go about it."

Yolanda wasn't too sure what she meant by an ad, but the others were so confident that it would result in a job for Papa that she let herself be convinced.

After the dishes were washed and put away, she gathered up her homework. Mrs. Debney had asked her to sit with the children that evening while she attended a meeting.

The Debneys lived a block away, and their house was much larger than Aunt Connie's. It was more elegantly furnished, too, with a large color television, instead of a small black-and-white set, softer chairs and sofas, and even a machine that washed dishes so they did not have to be done by hand. Baby-sitting for many people had taught Yolanda that Aunt Connie's neat little house was not luxurious by Anglo standards. It was small and plain, but she loved it just the same.

Mrs. Debney was dressing when she arrived, and her two small children were already in bed.

"But they aren't asleep," added their mother. "At least Susan's still awake. She wants you to read her a story. Do you mind?"

164

Yolanda didn't mind. She went to the children's room, sat down on the bed and began to read *Peter Rabbit*. She read softly in order not to disturb Jennie, asleep in the other twin bed. Above her own low voice, she could hear Mrs. Debney humming in the next room. Both wall ventilators must be open. Sometimes the Debneys kept them that way so they could hear the children if they stirred in the night.

After *Peter Rabbit*, Susan demanded a second book. Yolanda had just begun *The Three Bears* when she heard a new voice in the next room.

"Your door was unlocked, so I walked in. Goodness, Ruth. Aren't you ready yet?"

"I won't be a minute, Alice. Sit down," said Mrs. Debney.

Yolanda recognized the other voice now. It was Mrs. Haynes. She had done baby sitting for her, too, but Mrs. Haynes wasn't as nice as Mrs. Debney. She always acted as though she were doing Yolanda a favor when she paid for her services, and she never said thank-you for sitting with the children.

"Who's sitting for you?" asked Mrs. Haynes.

"Yolanda Ruiz."

"Yolanda's pretty good. But it means you'll have to get home early. Her aunt's so fussy. I've got Helen Patterson. She can stay later."

"Helen spends most of her time on the phone," objected Mrs. Debney. "I'm not sure she even listens for the children. I'd rather have Yolanda."

Yolanda felt a glow of pride. She knew she shouldn't be listening to the voices coming through the ventilator. It was eavesdropping, which wasn't nice. She tried to concentrate on the book, but she had read Susan the story so often she knew it by heart.

"The Mexicans do make good servants," said Mrs. Haynes. "And they're fine for farm labor. If we just don't get too many of them. I heard today that Yolanda's father is trying to find a job here. We can't have that, Ruth. The Indians from the reservation are bad enough, filling up our schools the way they do. But at least after they're here awhile, some of them realize their place and drop out."

"Alice!" interrupted Mrs. Debney. "Hush! She's in the next room."

"The door's closed. I looked," said Mrs. Haynes carelessly. "It's just what I've always said. You let one or two families in and they bring their friends. We've got—"

There was a click as Mrs. Debney slammed shut the ventilators in her room.

Yolanda finished the story automatically. Mrs. Debney opened the door and whispered that they were leaving but that she would be home by ten. Yolanda nodded without looking up.

When she was sure they were gone, she walked down the hall into the living room. More than once she had played a make-believe game about this room, imagining that it belonged to her. Now the thick rugs, the soft davenports and chairs, the color television set were hateful objects. They were gringo luxuries, and she wanted no part of them.

Her school books were on the coffee table, but she didn't open them.

She had thought this was such a nice town, where the people were all friendly. Now she wondered what they had been saying behind her back. They probably said the same things about Aunt Connie and Mark and Debbie, too. Yolanda wondered if they knew. Debbie had once told her that some of the people here were snobbish. It hadn't seemed to bother her, but it bothered Yolanda. She was hurt by it. She hoped Papa wouldn't find a job in Trent. She didn't want to live where people were pleasant to your face and said mean things behind your back.

She tried to imagine some terrible punishment for Mrs. Haynes, like the one she had devised for Kelly in the berry fields. Somehow she couldn't do it. Mrs. Haynes was too self-assured, too perfect for anything to happen to her. She was the true gringo who looked down on all Mexican-Americans. Probably all the other people in the town felt the same inside and just didn't show it.

She was still sitting there, feeling miserable, when Mrs. Debney returned.

"Is it ten o'clock?" Yolanda scrambled awkwardly to her feet. She was careful not to raise her eyes.

"No," said Mrs. Debney. "I left early. It's only nine. But I'll pay you for the three hours anyway."

"No." Yolanda bent down to gather up her untouched school work. "I came at seven. That's two hours."

"Yolanda." Mrs. Debney's voice was strained. "You heard, didn't you? You heard what Alice Haynes said?"

"Yes." For the first time she looked Mrs. Debney full in the face. "I heard."

"I knew it. That's why I came home early, to talk to you. Yolanda, you mustn't judge the whole town by one person. Or even by a few. They're in the minority, and it's ignorance on their part. The majority of us don't feel that way about your people or about the Indians either. We know that you have the same rights that we have, and that you're just as good. It's the bigots who make the loudest noise. Sometimes it's easier to seem to listen than to argue with them. But we don't have to agree."

The hard lump inside of Yolanda's chest turned over, but it didn't melt. She hoped Mrs. Debney was telling the truth, that she didn't think the way Mrs. Haynes did.

"It's all right," she said unhappily.

"I hope your father does find a job here," said Mrs. Debney. "I want you to stay."

"I don't want to stay," Yolanda told her. "Our home is Tierra Agreste."

She was careful to say nothing about Mrs. Haynes when she got back to Aunt Connie's, but she did admit that she hadn't finished her homework. Aunt Connie let her stay up a little later, and with the security of the familiar walls about her, she was able to complete her math.

It was lucky that she did, for when Miss Sparrow gave her the following day's assignment, she said it would be their last session together.

"This is the day's lesson for the regular fifth grade. Do the problems and take them to class tomorrow. You'll be up with the others," she said, smiling.

"But I can't be. We only started in September."

"You're a good student," praised Miss Sparrow. "You've worked very hard, and we've been doubling up. One student working with one teacher can progress much faster than one teacher and thirty students."

"And when I go home, they can't send me back to the fourth grade?"

"No. When you leave you'll have your report card with all your grades marked on it. But perhaps you won't have to go," suggested Miss Sparrow. "I hear that your father might find a job and that you'll stay here with us."

Yolanda stared at her in amazement. How could Miss Sparrow have heard that? Mrs. Haynes had known too. The news must be all over town.

"No," she said flatly. "We'll go home. We don't

belong here. We are Mexican-American. This is an Anglo town."

"Oh?" Miss Sparrow's black eyebrows lifted in surprise. "Then I don't belong here either. I am one-quarter Indian. My grandmother is a full-blooded Cheyenne."

"You are part Indian?" Yolanda stared at the black hair, twisted in a smart knot, at the brown eyes, the creamy olive skin, the tweed suit, and the beaded pendant hanging above the white blouse.

"Yes, indeed." Miss Sparrow nodded emphatic-ally. "I applied at this school hoping to get the seventh grade so I would work with the children from the reservation. There was no opening in the seventh, but there was in the fourth. I took that instead."

"Does Mr. Robinson know? And the teachers?"

"Of course. Many of the children as well. They probably don't think it's worth mentioning. You see, it's not an Anglo town, Yolanda. It's an American town. You and I are Americans. When someone resents us, it's better to ignore them. There are more who will accept us for ourselves."

Yolanda nodded, unconvinced. It was something she would have to think about. But Miss Sparrow was a teacher, and teachers were smart. Smarter than Mrs. Haynes. Moreover, Miss Sparrow was part-Indian and seemed proud of it. She had never re-alized that a part-Indian could become an accepted teacher. She would have to think about that, too.

On Thursday, Aunt Connie's ad appeared in the weekly paper. It proved to be a notice in a special column about people who were looking for jobs. Papa's was not the only one, but it was the best. It was a fine ad, and anyone who read it could tell that he was an outstanding person. He was honest, responsible, and hard-working. He was experienced in livestock and farming, but he would consider anything that was honorable and paid a living wage.

All evening they waited for the phone to ring.

"Lots of people don't get around to reading the paper the day it comes out," said Aunt Connie, when it was bedtime and there hadn't been one call. "Maybe tomorrow."

But there was no response to the ad the next day or the next. Aunt Connie told the paper to run it the following week, but Yolanda knew it was no use. There were probably too many people like Mrs. Haynes in Trent.

She didn't know whether to be happy or sad. She was no longer bitter, but she would never baby-sit for Mrs. Haynes again. Both Miss Sparrow and Mrs. Debney said it was better to ignore such people. Half of her said it would be nice to stay and not have to go up the road again. The other half kept insisting that Tierra Agreste was home—her real friends were there.

She had stopped praying to Our Lady to find Papa

a job. Our Lady would do whatever was best, and Yolanda would accept her decision.

The Sunday before Thanksgiving, Aunt Connie packed another dinner to take to camp. On the chance that someone still might answer the ad, they waited until the last possible minute before setting out; finally, Aunt Connie said they might as well leave. No one was going to call.

"I feel like I'm going to a funeral," she confessed. "I'll have to tell Alvaro there aren't any jobs. I blame myself for the whole thing. I should never have mentioned it in the first place."

It was growing dusk by the time they drove into camp. Aunt Connie parked the car and gave each of the children something to carry in.

Since only adults and older children worked in the potatoes, the alleys between the cabins were alive with younger ones. Larger boys played ball, small ones had originated their own game of kick-the-can. Girls, wrapped in rebozos, stood around in little groups, talking and gossiping.

Everyone stopped to watch the visitors getting from the car. As they approached, Rosie left one of the groups and came running toward Yolanda.

"Is it true?" she demanded. "Roberto says you are going to stay here and not go back to Tierra Agreste?"

"No," said Yolanda. "It is not true. We are going back."

173

"Oh!" Rosie turned and hurried back to her friends.

Yolanda looked after her resentfully. Rosie might have said something besides "Oh!" She could have said she was glad they were going home with her or that she was sorry Papa couldn't find a job. Anything would have been better than just "Oh!"

When they returned from the fields, Mama and Papa brought the news that three more days of work would finish the harvest.

"Everyone is very happy," said Papa. "It is a good year for potatoes. They are thankful that the crop is in before their holiday."

"Did you find Papa a job?" demanded Roberto, and Mama frowned at him for his rudeness. Roberto should have left such an important question to the grownups.

"No," admitted Aunt Connie sadly. "We tried everywhere, Alvaro. We ran an ad in the paper and asked everyone we knew. There is nothing open right now."

"You were kind to try," said Papa courteously. "I hope it was not too much inconvenience."

Yolanda glanced around at her family. Papa's expression had not changed. Perhaps he had not expected anything of this and had only agreed to please Aunt Connie. Mama could not hide her relief. It would be hard for her to leave her old friends, to live in a strange town where she could not even speak the language. For a moment Roberto looked disappointed, but he recovered quickly.

"If we stayed, I would have to leave Albert, and Albert is my best friend," he said. "I hope no one gets home ahead of us. I would hate to miss the homecoming fiesta."

Tomas said nothing, but he smiled. Yolanda knew that he was glad to be returning to Pablo Galindez and the other Chicanos.

"There is no reason for you to go," insisted Aunt Connie quickly. "My house is small, but it is larger than this cabin. There will be room for all of us when the camp closes down for the winter. We can keep looking. Something will turn up."

"No," said Papa. "Such a thing would not be right. I must be master in my own home. I could not impose on you in such a way. Without a job and my own house, we must return."

"There is work in the mint," argued Aunt Connie. "They have planted the roots and must plow them under for protection."

"How long will it take?" he asked suspiciously.

Aunt Connie had to admit that it was not long, but in the early spring, she added hastily, work would begin again. The mint must be fertilized, and when it came up, there would be hoeing, much hoeing. The children could help with that on weekends. It would go on until the thick carpet had grown to cover the ground.

Yolanda held her breath, listening intently. Aunt Connie sounded very persuasive.

When she had finished, Papa shook his head.

"There are the months in between," he reminded her. "Long months in which to do nothing. We will go home to spend those idle months. Here, we would have to find a house to live in, and the rent would be high. Food would be more expensive. No, it is not to be. We are migrants. When it is time, we must go up the road."

15

Yolanda had never smelled anything like Aunt
Connie's house that Thanksgiving Day. Mr.
Teal had given each of his employees a turkey, and
now Aunt Connie's was roasting in the oven. The
whole house smelled of turkey and dressing, of
pumpkin and mince pies, of pickles newly taken
from their sealed jars, and of yeast rolls. They were
smells she would always remember.

It was the last time they would be together; tomorrow they would start up the road. The potato
harvest was finished the day before Thanksgiving,
but Aunt Connie had persuaded them to delay their
departure until the day after so they could cele-
brate this Anglo holiday.

Now, as she helped set the table, Yolanda almost
wished they hadn't stayed. It wasn't being a very
happy day.

Mama was uneasy about the trip home and kept

talking about the terrible things that could happen. They had never traveled on their own before. It had always been in a truck with many people and a leader who knew the road.

Papa was not concerned with their travels, but his mind seemed to be far away—perhaps on the job they had been unable to find for him—and he did not make little jokes the way he always did at a fiesta.

Aunt Connie tried to smile, but she could not hide her disappointment; and Debbie went about sniffing openly.

As for Yolanda herself, now that it was time to leave, she almost wished that Our Lady had willed them to stay. It was hard to give up this comfortable house with the luxuries they would never have at home. She would miss her school, her classmates, and the teachers who had been so kind. It was hardest of all to say good-by to Aunt Connie and Debbie and Mark.

Only her brothers seemed untouched by sadness this Thanksgiving. In the living room Tomas, Roberto, Lennie, and Mark were sitting on the floor in front of the television, lost to everything else.

"Perhaps Luis was not so foolish as we thought," said Papa. Oddly enough, he was not interested in television today. He had joined the women in the kitchen, something Yolanda had never seen him do before. "Luis turned his back on the *raza*—his own people—and took up with the ways of the gringo. But his widow and children will never know hunger. I could not say the same."

"He did not turn his back in all ways." Aunt Connie glanced at the Madonna, resting in her little shrine against the wall. "His people were very dear to Louie, and it was his greatest wish to help them He said the only way was through education. Did you know that Louie had learned to read and write?"

Papa shook his head. He looked surprised.

"I helped him in the beginning, but most of it he did himself. Every night he read the newspaper so he could learn what was going on in the world. He was very strict with Debbie and Mark. If they brought home a bad grade, Louie was angry."

"But why?" asked Papa. "Why did it mean so much?"

"Today we live in an Anglo world," explained Aunt Connie. "But it will not always be that way. Someday the brown, the black, the red men will have equal voices, but only if the words they speak are worth listening to. They cannot be words of hate and anger. They must be calm and filled with wisdom. Learning comes from education, and that is what Louie wanted for his children."

"Luis was a dreamer," said Papa tolerantly. "Such a thing could never be. Not for a Mexican-American."

"Until you came here and saw how we lived, you would not have believed that, either," she reminded him. "This, too, was Louie's dream, and it came true."

It was plain that Papa did not want to continue this conversation. He left the room abruptly and joined the boys at the television, but Yolanda noticed that above the black eyebrows his forehead was slightly wrinkled. He was thinking of the things Aunt Connie had said.

After the dinner dishes were washed and put away, the family got into the station wagon to return to camp. This time Yolanda and Maria went too. They would be leaving early the next morning.

Aunt Connie, Debbie, and Mark shivered in the cold wind at the curb, waving good-by.

"Don't go," wailed Debbie. "Oh, Yolanda, it's going to be so lonesome without you!"

"Write me a letter, Maria," shrieked Mark. "I never had a letter in the mail. Put my name on it."

"I will keep looking. If a job opens up, I will let you know," called Aunt Connie. "But come back for the potatoes, anyway. Petra, make him come back for the potatoes next year."

Papa gunned the motor, then let it idle.

"We will come for the mint," he announced. "Look for us early in the spring. Then my children can go to your school."

Yolanda saw Aunt Connie smile and turn to interpret the remark to Debbie. She herself could hardly believe that she was hearing right. Sometimes, in the spring, they did not bother to enroll in school. The truant officers had relaxed their vigilance by then, and, after all, what were a few weeks?

"Oh, Yolanda," cried Debbie in excitement. "I'll tell Old Lady Hog. She'll be glad."

"They will not be as I am," declared Papa firmly. "My children will have a better life. In school, they will learn how to do this. Luis was right, and I was wrong."

He stepped on the gas.

It was dark by the time they drove into camp. Most of the cabins were deserted because the occupants had gone as soon as the last potato sack had been delivered to the warehouse. Tomorrow everything would be closed down for the year.

Light came from the windows of the Corona cabin, and as soon as Mama got out of the car, she turned to Roberto.

"Tell the Coronas we are home," she ordered. "Tell them to come to our house. Tonight we will have a fiesta, with such good things to eat, they will never believe."

Aunt Connie had insisted on sending all the leftovers—the turkey and cranberries, the salad, the rolls, and slices of pie. She said they would make a good lunch on their journey, but Yolanda agreed that it was better to share with their friends right now. After all, the Coronas should have Thanksgiving, too.

She helped carry the boxes into the cabin and carefully hung the new blue coat on a nail behind one of the beds. It was chilly inside, but with so many people eating she was afraid something might be spilled on it.

The Coronas lost no time accepting the invitation. They crowded into the cabin and began exclaiming over the food spread out on the table.

"It is yours," Mama told them, happy that she could provide pleasure for her friends.

Rosie was the last to arrive. She walked in quietly, wrapped in her old green rebozo, and her eyes searched the room for Yolanda. When they found her, she smiled hesitantly. Yolanda squeezed past Roberto and Albert to join her.

"Hi," she said, and didn't realize until she heard her own voice that she sounded exactly like Debbie and the Anglos in school.

"*Hola,*" said Rosie briefly.

"Help yourself before the boys get it all." This time Yolanda spoke in Spanish. "The turkey is good. Have that little slice of mince pie, too, before somebody else gets it."

"You will not take anything?" asked Rosie politely.

"I have eaten," Yolanda told her, shrugging. She would have liked the pie, but she didn't need it.

Her stomach was still full enough from dinner.

Rosie ate the pie without saying how good it was and started on a slice of turkey. People kept crowding around the table, sampling this and that, and the food began to disappear. Their conversation and laughter echoed back and forth between the walls in a great roar that made it hard to hear.

"Fill a plate for yourself, and we can go outside," suggested Yolanda finally. "It is a nice night. All the stars are shining."

"But it is cold," Rosie reminded her, as she squeezed in once more to the table.

The new blue coat was clear across the room. To reach it, Yolanda would have to climb over Grandmother Corona, Lennie, and the youngest Corona boys, who were sitting on the bed. She left it where it was, and took her mother's black reboza, which was easier to reach.

"Where is your fine coat?" asked Rosie, as they stepped outside.

"Hanging on a nail." Yolanda took deep breaths of fresh air. It smelled of frost, and the ground beneath her shoes was hard and unyielding.

"I like you better in that," said Rosie frankly. "You are again like yourself. Except for the shoes." Then she added brightly, "Papa is going to buy me new shoes. I can no longer push my feet into my old ones. They will go to my brother."

Yolanda looked down at the rusty folds of her

mother's rebozo and at Rosie's familiar green one, at the neat brown oxfords and the bare feet. Suddenly she knew why Rosie had been so stand-offish and strange. It wasn't fair for one person to live in a grand house and wear fine clothes while the other had nothing.

"Do you like our station wagon?" asked Rosie eagerly. "It is funny to see where we go and not always look back where we have been. When Papa drove us the first time, my brothers cried. They thought the cars coming would smash into us— bomp!"

"I was a little scared, too," admitted Yolanda. "I never rode facing the front until Papa bought Señor Oro's car."

"It didn't scare me," denied Rosie firmly, starting on a pickle.

Rosie would never admit being scared of anything, thought Yolanda, but inside she was just as frightened as anyone, particularly of new things she did not understand. It was as much a part of her nature as Yolanda's habit of making up stories. It didn't matter. Inside, Rosie was good.

"Do you like the pickle?" she asked.

"Um." Rosie didn't want to commit herself. She licked the juice from her fingers. "Did you eat these things all the time you were here?"

"Oh, no. Today is a fiesta. This is special food. We ate ordinary things on other days."

"Like tortillas and beans," supplied Rosie. "They are best after all. It will be a lean winter for us. Our papas spent so much money for the station wagon. But I am glad we are going home tomorrow. I do not like this place."

"There were things I did not like either," confessed Yolanda, remembering Mrs. Haynes. "Some of the people are not so nice."

"I warned you about those gringos." Rosie smiled smugly. "I guess you forgot."

"Some of them are good," insisted Yolanda loyally. "You would like them, too, Rosie, if you got to know them. How is Concha?"

"She was well when I saw her," Rosie's tone was a little defensive. "Concha is a good *chica*. She is a fast picker, too. She did almost as well as I did on the apples." She hesitated a moment before she added, "Concha may not be so glad to see you come home. She was my best friend after you left."

"I do not want anyone to feel that way," Yolanda said earnestly. "It is hard to be the odd person. Why not have two best friends instead of just one?"

Rosie agreed instantly. She seemed relieved that from now on Concha would be included.

The night wind was raising goose bumps on their arms, but they stayed on, shivering. It had been a long time since the two of them had talked together.

"How was your school? What was it like?" asked Yolanda. She knew Rosie wasn't interested in school, but it was something to prolong the conversation.

"Who knows? They are all the same. They asked me what grade I was in, and when I told them, they did not argue. It was easy."

"I am in the fifth grade now," Yolanda told her. Rosie would have to know. She had a note from Mr. Robinson to the teacher in Tierra Agreste, as well as the fifth grade report card showing her marks for the first three months.

"You should not count on it," Rosie looked at her anxiously. She was fast becoming her old self again. "It does not matter what grade you are in. Do not worry if they put you back. When you get too old for school, you stop going. And the fifth grade is not so much."

No, it wasn't so much, Yolanda agreed silently. But after the fifth grade there was the sixth, and the seventh, and the eighth.

She pictured herself two years from now arriving at school and announcing that she was only fourteen years old. She imagined the consternation on the faces of the teachers when they realized they would have to start a seventh grade in Tierra Agreste just for her.

"You have not changed as much as I thought you had," said Rosie, laughing tolerantly. "You have that funny look on your face again."